Praise for *(Don't) Call Mum*

"Matt Wesolowski is one of the UK's best horror writers – *(Don't) Call Mum* is impossible to put down. Unmissable for horror fans (and any one with taste)."
Eliza Clark, author of *She's Always Hungry*

"All the Wesolowski gifts are here: strong writing, intense setting, unsettling themes, and a unique slant on horror. This is modern, thrilling, clever, and I bloody loved it!" **Louise Beech, author of *Nothing Else* and *I Am Dust***

"Matt Wesolowski at his very best: dark humour, sinister folklore and lurking horror. It builds from the seemingly banal to a disturbing climax that lingers long after you've finished reading. Brilliantly unsettling."
Guy Morpuss, author of *A Trial in Three Acts* and *Black Lake Manor*

"The perfect bite-size piece of Northern dread. With its grim British folkloric threats brought to life in an expertly conjured (and equally bleak) modern-day setting, you'll be unable to disembark this train ride of the damned." **Ally Wilkes, author of *Where the Dead Wait* and *All the White Spaces***

"Wesolowski skilfully layers modern storytelling with grim folklore to leave readers haunted by dread. (Don't) Call Mum is eerie, tense, and will have you breathless by the final stop." **Tanya Pell, author of *CICADA***

"*(Don't) Call Mum* is pristine Wesolowski. Claustrophobic, taut, and achingly unnerving, the story unfolds much like the train car the characters find themselves on - barrelling along while the shadows move closer to the windows. Ultimately, this is something you'll pick up and not be able to put down, and you'll realize that throughout, you've had to remind yourself to breathe. This was spectacular." **Steve Stred, author of *Mastodon* and *Churn the Soil***

(DON'T) CALL MUM

"A slice of true Northern terror. Matt Wesolowski perfectly captures the dark beyond the window of the local train and fills it with nightmares." **Oliver K Langmead, author of *Calypso* and *Glitterati***

"Wesolowski's atmospheric and chilling tale will haunt you. The way he weaves folklore into a modern-day setting is masterfully done. A cracking read." **Tendai Huchu, author of the *Edinburgh Nights* series**

(Don't) Call Mum

Matt Wesolowski

WILD HUNT BOOKS

(Don't) Call Mum
First published in 2025 by Wild Hunt Books
wildhuntbooks.co.uk

Copyright © 2025 by Matt Wesolowski
Matt Wesolowski asserts the moral right to be identified as the author of this work.

All rights reserved. No part of this publication may be reproduced, stored or transmitted in any form or by any means, electronic, mechanical, photocopying, recording, scanning, or otherwise without written permission from the publisher, except for brief quotation for review. No part of this book may be used or reproduced in any manner for the purpose of training artificial intelligence technologies, generative AI or other artificial intelligence systems. It is illegal to copy this book, post it to a website, or distribute it by any other means without permission.

This novel is entirely a work of fiction. The names, characters and incidents portrayed in it are the work of the author's imagination. Any resemblances to actual persons, living or dead, events or localities are entirely coincidental.

A CIP catalogue record for this title is available from the British Library

Paperback: 978-1-7394580-4-1
Ebook: 978-1-7394580-5-8

Cover Design by Luísa Dias
Edited by Ariell Cacciola
Typeset by Wild Hunt Books

The Northern Weird Project is a registered trademark of Wild Hunt Books

Remembering Paul Clark

The Midlands
90 Miles North of London

SHE'S TALKING LOUDLY ENOUGH so the entire platform can hear her. A crow's caw against the burr of gathered people noise.

"I know it's true because I'm *basically* an historian."

She adds a dash of laughter to her vowels.

Historia-ah-ah-ahn

Leo immediately can't stand her.

Condensation appears above a little coven of students on the platform edge joined by the occasional puffs of vape smoke that rise up in bubble gum-flavoured geysers. The boys have mullets, bad moustaches, shell-suit tops and baseball caps. This one woman doing all the talking is an earnest goth with a septum piercing and an unnecessarily huge pair of glasses.

Sweet summer children, Leo thinks as the gap between under- and post-grad opens up like a chasm between them and him.

Leo has chosen to fill this chasm with his derision.

He's not even sorry.

Leo pulls his not-warm-enough jacket around himself and nuzzles into his scarf. Back when he was a first year, waiting at this exact platform at this exact station to go home for Christmas, he wore a band T-shirt and smoked a cigarette – a hangover drawn around him like a habit.

Right now, he just wants to go home in peace.

"When people talk about witches," the loud woman is saying, "it's all, *Salem, Salem, Salem,* but no one ever mentions, like, the thirty people that were hanged for witchcraft up on Newcastle Town Moor."

Her earnestness isn't lost on Leo.

His lip curls in a sneer.

New-*cars*-el

Everyone else on the platform huddles closer together because of the cold. This station sits in the middle of the country in the space between North and South.

The wind barrels through in a bad temper. It ripples coats and snatches at scarves. Occasionally, someone will take a step forward and peer down the empty lines as if willpower alone will summon a train. Leo shuffles his feet, toes already going numb.

A raucous peal of too-loud laughter from the students turns a few heads.

Leo glares. He's definitely not bitter; these kids with their whole academic lives ahead of them. Not having fucked it all up yet.

Nope, not bitter at all.

We were all first years once, Leo thought. *We all had that wide-eyed notion that we knew everything after attending a couple of lectures.*

Leo watches the 'historian' for a while. A prophet in her leather trench coat and her glasses with the thick, look-at-me frames, regaling her disciples. Most of them look impressed. He hopes she's not getting the same train as him.

Another peal of laughter and Leo shakes his head, but he can't help smiling.

Time moves quick, kids, he thinks. *Blink and you're suddenly a post-grad with no direction, pulling pints of piss on the campus bar to pay your fees...*

Leo blows out his own plume of condensation and stares around the station, trying to not think about the first years. Pigeons force themselves into the eaves of ancient girders as a baleful icy wind cuts through Leo's jacket. His trainers have grit stuck in the treads. His suitcase drips slush-water onto the platform. Clothes and books scrunched up tight together for the journey North.

Leo turns back to them, a pang of guilt spreading through his stomach. Who is he to judge this lot anyway? We were all that insufferable once. An errant memory surfaces again, drives its blade between his ribs, curls his toes. Leo full of cheap lager and sugary shots in Freshers Week. He was staggering, drunkenly trying to explain the intricacies of Nick Cave lyrics to a bored woman in the campus bar he now works behind.

The throb of music, the smell of sweat and perfume. Laughter and the rattle of ice in a plastic cup. Leo was sat too close to her, booze blinding him to the fact that the poor woman just wanted to be left alone. His eager tongue was wrestling with his words.

'*Brompton Oratory is literally about Cave breaking up with PJ Harvey. The Catholic imagery in that song is so fucking profound...*'

Her half-smile and eyes that looked past him and said, *help*. A tiny white fleck of his spit on her cheek. She pretended not to notice before turning away and wiping it with the back of her hand.

Brutal.

Leo rifles through his rucksack for his ear buds; pulls out his phone and starts his music. It fills his head and his heart with delicious fury; Bleed From Within. Full blast. Leo opens the live departures app.

Leo's train is surprisingly on time. The app shows a troubling array of red 'delayed' or 'cancelled' alerts for many of the other routes and Leo feels a little bit smug. For him this is a familiar journey: a couple of hours north, one change at York, then up, up, up into the wilds, past the bright lights of Newcastle-Upon-Tyne. Goodbye to the last big city and on into the welcome wilderness of home.

Home is where patchwork fields reach the horizon. Brooding hills in the distance. Sheep farms and cobbled streets. Malacstone. Northumberland.

Leo messages his mam.

> Train is on time…incredible scenes!

She answers with a big, yellow thumbs-up.

He hopes she'll light the log fire and order Chinese tonight in celebration of her only child's return. Mam's looked tired lately; she keeps asking Leo if he's going to apply to teacher training college to get a 'proper job' after his master's.

You can't work in a bar forever.

Leo wants to tell her that he's hoping his dissertation, 'The Cottingley Fairies Impact on Folkloric Belief in the Early 20th Century', will somehow blow up and allow him to spend the rest of his days being paid to potter around in some ancient library.

But he doesn't.

Leo wonders if any of his mates might be about tonight; he floats a suggestion in the World Class Wrecking Cru WhatsApp Group.

> *Getting in tonight if anyone's down for a pint?*

A few of them see it but no one replies. They're all farmers, all still working, spreading straw through the barns, repairing the dry stonewalls by the light of their head torches.

Leo's hands have started feeling the cold again since he came down here to uni; *Going soft, you lad,* the boys say to him when he pulls on gloves.

Leo's headphones give a little bleep and die.

He lets out a sigh but keeps them in his ears, so no one will try and talk to him.

Leo picks up a free newspaper from a puddle of slush and reads it just so he isn't alone with the sound of his brain.

The headlines surge with the same story. That bloke that went missing last week. His tearful kids. On the next page, a double feature about who's going to be in the next series of *I'm a Celebrity...*

Leo leans back against a pillar; the bricks are cold on his spine, when a voice rises, cutting through his nerves.

"I've actually started an online campaign for a memorial to commemorate them, you know? Those people from Newcastle *wrongly accused of witchcraft.*"

The historian's voice is high and excruciating.

"They should plant it on the Town Moor up there," she says. "I believe those people should, like, never be forgotten."

Leo watches from over his newspaper, the rest of the students nodding and checking their phones.

"Liked. Shared," some of them say.

Slacktivists, Leo thinks. *Post about issues on socials in lieu of actually doing anything.*

Leo turns the page of his newspaper from stories of bombs falling on innocent civilians to a feature on how to make your holiday more 'Insta-licious'.

There's a sudden blast of feedback and everyone on the platform collectively cowers.

"The next train approaching Platform Five," comes crackling out of the Tannoy, "is the four-fifteen service to York."

The announcement dissolves into a squeal of feedback and the crowd of waiting passengers begin shuffling closer to the platform edge. Leo discards the newspaper and follows suit.

The front cover looks back at him balefully; the missing man's family haven't given up hope. Leo turns away and looks down the line for the train.

You were never cut out to be a farmer, love. Mam sometimes tells him and there's a grin on her face and in her eyes. Leo saw that grin replaced by tears when he got accepted to his undergrad and had wished dad had been around to see it, too. When she hugged him, the bones of her back felt brittle. Bird-like. All that remains of dad today is the waxy overcoat that mam can't bear to take down from the peg in the hall, still stained with mud from top field.

The undergrads are saying their goodbyes.

Home comforts are waiting for each of them; hugs and kisses; warm childhood beds with clean sheets.

Another blast of whistling feedback.

"There has been a platform alteration."

There is a collective muttering from Platform Six.

"At least it's not a delay!" Someone says.

The Tannoy gives another whistle.

"The four twenty-five service to London Kings Cross will now depart from Platform Eleven B."

The muttering turns to groans.

Platform Eleven B is over the other side of the station. People are already speed-walking that way, suitcases growling behind them.

"Oh, for fuck's sake! Eleven B is *miles away!*" says the Historian to her friends. "Ok, babes. I gotta go. Love you, love you mwah, mwah."

She scurries past Leo toward the bridge. Black trench coat flapping. She's off south. So much for caring about the ghosts of witches on Newcastle Town Moor.

"I bet she's got a micro-Z tattoo behind her ear and spends most of summer trying to hide it."

Leo whips around at the voice.

"Or is that reference out of date now?" A woman has sidled up to him and is grinning, shrugging her shoulders. She's around Leo's age. Retro-looking army-style overcoat, yellow beanie.

"Ha," Leo says, dry as possible, hiding his surprise. "Right? How long did it take her to realise it was a Nazi symbol?"

The woman in the yellow hat and Leo stare after the first year who is struggling up the stairs with her suitcase, and New Rock boots glinting.

"Oh, ages," Yellow Hat says. "Definitely tells everyone it was deliberate and 'actually reclaimed now, yeah?'"

Her accent is definitely North East, but with wider diphthongs than a Geordie. Maybe Sunderland, Hartlepool.

Wheys keys Lou-eyse.

"Have they changed the fucking York train platform by the way?" she says.

"No," Leo says. "None of this soft, southern platform change nonsense round 'ere."

Yellow Hat smiles. This is weird, Leo thinks. Women don't just come and talk to him like this unless they're asking him to pull them a pint.

"Ah, right," Yellow Hat says. "Cheers, mate."

She takes a few steps just outside of talking range and pulls out her phone.

Leo scours his imagination for a reason to go over and talk to her.

He thinks better of it and stays put.

"The train approaching Platform Five," the Tannoy suddenly proclaims, "is the four-fifteen service to York."

More people begin shuffling toward the platform edge, crowding. A few of the pigeons clatter from their positions on the girders and vanish into the roof of the station. Leo picks up the handle of his suitcase; it's time to decide his position.

Leo has a game that he plays against himself on train journeys. The object of the game is to try and stand on a place on the platform that faces the door straight-on when the train stops. The rule is, that you have to choose your position on the platform before the nose of the approaching train passes the far end of the platform. Then you have to commit to it. You wait until the train reaches a full halt and you win if you only have to walk straight forward to the door. A single step right or left is a fail.

He's only ever managed it once.

There's a rumble and the train snakes around a corner breaking with a slow whine. Leo takes a few steps to his right. Yellow Hat is still here.

Here's the deal, Leo says inside his head. *If you win the game, you're allowed to make some passing comment to her as you board the train. Nothing creepy. If you lose, you have to forget she ever existed.*

Done.

Leo commits to his position on the platform and waits.

North Yorkshire
200 Miles North of London

LEO DEPARTS AT YORK station. A huge, listed building where pale pillars hold up gilded iron over a terminal of rust-coloured rails.

If the Midlands are England's diaphragm, York is its heart. Hundreds of routes north, southeast and west sprout from here like steel-railed arteries.

Leo's train North East to Malacstone gets two platform alterations in five minutes which is a whole world of bullshit. Leo is sweating when he eventually reaches the platform furthest from the shops and toilets. Platform Fourteen.

Here, the weather screams in, a freezing wind and the edges of rain. It's darker too now, the afternoon rushing out of sight like a runaway carriage, slipping away without a sunset.

Fourteen looks like a spare platform, only for use in emergencies. A blank brick wall and a single wooden bench. No billboards advertising celebrity-penned novels or warnings about bag theft.

The display board on Platform Fourteen is, of course, blank and Leo frets, checking his phone to make sure that the train due in a few minutes will take him home. The rest of the station has been chaos; trains are going down one after another; delays and cancellations; hordes of passengers swelling on the larger platforms. Leo, for once is glad he has to take the rickety Northern Sprinter service out into the middle-of-nowhere Northumberland.

"Excuse me, mate." A red-faced man with a mod style haircut pushed over his forehead strides over.

"This is the seven-forty to Birmingham mate, yeah?" Sausage roll and Carling breath in Leo's face.

He points at the fume-stained brickwork behind the empty tracks.

"I don't think so," Leo says.

"What?" The man says. "Fucking hell mate. Is this not Platform Ten?"

Leo tries not to look at the sign but assures the man this is Fourteen and attempts a smile.

The man scowls.

Leo wants to apologise.

"Fine," the man says, turning around. "I'll fucking just go up another fucking flight of fucking stairs, shall I?"

Leo watches the man stomp off, shaking his head and swearing as he goes.

"Oi, you. Is this Platform Six?"

Leo yelps and whips around.

It's the woman with the yellow hat. She's out of breath and hat-less, revealing a close-cropped undercut. Her top lip is beaded with sweat.

"Jesus," Leo says. "Just shat myself."

She's laughing.

"Are you getting the Sprinter up into nowhere as well, I take it?" she says.

"Shh." Leo puts a hand to his lips and lowers his voice and says, "So far it's the only one that's running on time. Don't jinx it."

Yellow Hat grins and backs up a bit, turning her smile toward the emptiness of the platform.

Leo searches for something witty to say, something that'll keep her here. It looks like they're the only two people getting this service, and a little part of Leo hopes it'll stay that way.

"The train approaching Platform Fourteen," says the Tannoy, "is the six-twenty Northern Sprinter service to Ellie Hill calling at Newcastle-Upon-Tyne, Dunston, Wylam, Riding Mill, Corbridge, Underwood, Darkton, Colliwell, Malacstone..."

Spilling through the platform entrance is a gaggle of other passengers, eyes wide and faces red. A few of them are pointing to the big Platform Fourteen sign.

"Brace yourself," Leo says out of the corner of his mouth, "to be asked whether this is Platform Fourteen and whether the train that is coming is a train that indeed goes along tracks and takes people to stations."

There are no reserved seats on this train. The Northern Sprinter is a direct contrast to its sleek, red cousins that zip up and down the country with their pointed noses and onboard coffee.

The Sprinter's two carriages smell of diesel fumes and feet. Their doors rattle and joints squeak as they lumber through the darkness, the cold air seeping in under their doors and the peeling rubber seal around their windows. Vents next to every seat belch out warm bad breath.

Despite all this, Leo has an odd sense of protectiveness about the train; yes, it's a bit shit, decrepit, forgotten and underfunded but it's familiar. It's a little slice of home.

Leo's sat in the middle of the carriage. Yellow Hat is sitting a few seats in front with her back to Leo, reading a book. She's the only other person here.

Leo's playing, *I wonder what she's reading and then I'll judge her for it* and keeps trying to get a glimpse of the cover when she raises it up to turn the page. Is he going to walk over and try and discuss literature with a lone woman on a desolate train?

Shy bairns get nowt, they say where Leo's from.

But also, no.

Leo texts his mam.

> *On the last leg now. ETA about 9ish….Chinese? X*

He adds a smiley face, but the message doesn't send.

Something tickles against Leo's wrist. He looks down. One of the free newspapers has been folded tight like a concertina and shoved in the space between the window and the arm of the seat. He picks it up and tries to avoid the main story, but it unfolds like dusty, moth wings and he can't help but look.

'*Davey Hewitt: 5 Days gone*'

A blown-up photograph of a smiling face on the front, monstrous and deformed by the folds of the paper. Blotchy light; a bald head, a grin. Teeth and a blue shirt. Beer-brown eyes.

'Police accused of giving up in search for missing man...'

Leo swallows, throat suddenly hard.

Missing dad's daughter's plea to public...

A little girl in glasses. Mouth turned down.

'Don't give up on daddy.'

Leo folds the paper back up and replaces it. Careful like it's a relic. He turns to the window, stomach churning.

He's gone to Underwood.

This thought arrives in Leo's head without warning and lingers, clinging to the inside of his brain.

The train's engine splutters to life and the carriage doors wheeze closed. Leo watches the wall of the platform pull away then vanish into darkness as the night reaches out and encloses the train. The rattle of the engine is the familiar song of his journey home.

LEO'S FOREHEAD IS COLD against the glass. He watches through the window as the last remnants of the city turns to countryside. Sometimes the land will undulate, a hill or wood, the ripple of a black cloak but mostly it's just flat fields. Sleep hovers above him ready to pounce.

The train begins to slow as the land rises. The fields and walls crumble to bushes and rocks. Leo's eyes flicker closed.

The vibration of the train seat becomes the rumble of mum's quad bike as they round up the sheep. Sun dapples the yawning hills in shades of brown and green.

The ear-splitting roar of a jet overhead on a too-hot afternoon.

The plop of rocks into a lake where Leo taught himself how to skim stones.

The peaks and troughs of his boyhood play out across the hills. A bruised sunset hanging heavily across the sky. Mud clings to his hands and dries under his fingernails. Little Leo watches it all dissolve in the hot water of a bath. The smell of straw engulfs him; he sees sudden pink; the slippery sinew of a newborn lamb.

As Leo dreams, his head lolls against the window.

He shouldn't have looked at that newspaper. The missing man's story tapped the lid of some old vault buried in Leo's subconscious. As he drifts deeper into slumber, the vault creaks open and out crawls a spectral memory that's been long dormant as the years have rumbled by.

Mam? Where's dad gone?

Mam's tears long rubbed dry on her cheeks. The black of a night sky outside. The crackle of the fire in the hearth downstairs. Nanna on the sofa beside her. Embers flaring in their eyes.

He's gone to Underwood, Leo. Now get back up those stairs and go to sleep.

Those words became blunted by the years, draped in uncertainty. Leo's never had the nerve to ask her exactly what happened.

He ran away south instead.

He's spent the days since looking for a father-shape emerging from the dark. Half-formed like a promise.

When mam mentions dad, it's in flurries. Bitterness spills into her voice like she's biting into a lemon.

Your dad left us because he was weak, pathetic. Waste of space. We're better off.

Then she turns her head to the hills.

The wind moans gently between them.

In these moments Leo feels the calm before a scream.

Leo's sworn he'll never be like dad, running off and never coming back. He and his mam just got on with it. They had no choice. Leo stood in the dark holding nails while mam fixed the lambing shed and Nanna dozed, fitful in her chair. All the while, the wind and the rain and the relentless struggle of the farm did its best to ruin what little that they had.

Nanna died before Leo left Malacstone. Leo's last memory of her was the hospital, her withered hand clutching his university acceptance letter.

A smile.

Her whispered words before she closed her eyes.

Stay away from Underwood, Leo love.

Now her secrets were scattered to the hills with her ashes.

When they did it – Leo and mam, dressed in their best – something was watching from the quiet of the hills. He could feel it, heaving itself from childhood and peering out at this goodbye.

This offering to the land.

Leo and mam kept on with the farm. Refused to relent. Sometimes, when Leo was alone in the fields, he could feel something coming, a shape from the woods, from the dark. It was wreathed in fog, feet sluicing through the sodden grass. Leo wouldn't look. He wouldn't move.

Dad can stay there in Underwood.

That had made mam smile.

Leo's sworn to himself that during one of these visits he'll sit down and chat properly with mam about dad. He's made this promise again and again, staggering through the early mornings midlands streets, on his way home from work or a night out; neither north nor south, a gaping hole in him where a father should be.

The wind of the Northumberland hills that snatched nanna's ashes is still writhing within him.

The scream of that wind becomes the grinding howl of brakes.

Leo flounders back into reality, the past dissolving as the train thunders to a stop.

The past spilling from his mind.

He closes his eyes, the scream of the breaks filling the carriage.

The train slows with a quake before eventually stopping completely.

The carriage is in sudden silence. Leo breathes out, the sound of it huge.

Night has come as he slept.

Leo stares through the window, his hands shaking.

What has come with the night?

It's fine, Leo thinks. *This happens all the time. There's a logical explanation.*

Sheep on the line.

A person.

There is a tonne of reasons why the train stopped like this, and they don't have to be bad.

The rain and the wind are buffeting the windows which suddenly seem horribly flimsy, loose teeth in black gums.

The woman without her yellow hat stands up in her seat, turns around to Leo.

"You ok there, mate?"

Leo gives a big thumbs-up, not trusting his voice.

"What's going on?" she says.

Leo shrugs at the same moment the interior lights of the train flicker once before reigniting. A millisecond of blackness.

"Er...That's not good," Yellow Hat says.

Leo agrees.

Not good at all.

Leo peers out of the window, his distorted ghost staring forlornly back. He cups his hands around his eyes, presses them to the glass and stares out into the gloom.

"Between here's, what? Darlington? Durham?" Yellow Hat calls out, looking at her phone. "Signal's a bit shit."

As if in response, the train judders, the lights flicker once more and the train begins to move. Sluggish, reluctant. Leo and Yellow Hat sway slightly, standing up in their seats.

"Panic over," Leo says. "Are you heading much further?"

"End of the line," she says. "Ellie Hill."

"Ellie Hill?" Leo says. "You're practically Scottish."

Yellow Hat frowns.

"On your way home for Christmas?" Leo asks. This has the same energy as asking a taxi driver if they've been busy on a Saturday night.

"No," she says. "I'm from Seaton Carew. Just visiting the missus for the Christmas break."

Say-ton Car-ew. At least he wasn't far off with the accent.

"You're a sheep farmer?" she says. "Knew it as soon as I saw you."

Leo laughs.

"How?" he says.

"You've got the look of a Malacstoner."

Leo acts offended and tells her that the village of Malacstone is a bustling and cosmopolitan metropolis.

"We have a butcher's shop that has pig heads in the window and there's a big standing stone in the village square that everyone gathers round to look at on Sundays. But only if we've said our prayers to the Great God Pan."

Yellow Hat laughs and then peers at him, head cocked.

"I think I know you from somewhere?"

Leo wonders if she's seen him dead-eyed and hung over behind the bar on campus, doling out shots to excitable groups of freshers in fancy dress.

He shrugs.

"That's it!" She says. "I do know you! I've seen you skulking around in the humanities department at uni. Is that what you're studying? Geography or something?"

"MA in folklore," Leo says. "As fascinating to others who don't do an MA in folklore as it sounds."

He hopes he doesn't sound like a wanker. Like the *historian* spaffing on about witches. He doesn't want to add that he's writing a dissertation on fairies.

"Oh, that's so cool!" Yellow Hat says.

Leo says it is cool. To be fair, he still doesn't mention the fairies, though.

"You?"

"Sociolinguistics," she says, doing a chef's kiss gesture with her fingers. "Same. Only interesting to those who know sociolinguistics."

Leo smiles. She tells him she's doing something to do with feminist linguistic theory. Leo nods and pretends he knows what that is.

They both sigh with relief as the train engine begins whirring,

"I'm Jodie." She stretches out her hand. Leo does the same from his end of the carriage and they both shake their empty hands up and down.

"Anyway," Jodie says. "Sorry to be weird and like, just start chatting shit to a random stranger but there's not that many of the North East crew at uni is there? It's all a load of posh kids from the home counties. They hear our accent and think we're there to wash the dishes."

"To be fair," Leo says, "us talking to each other on a train like this is adhering to the stereotype of Northerners being friendly."

Jodie laughs.

"Isn't it weird," Leo goes on, "that we get all nostalgic for a place we've been spending most of our lives trying to escape from?"

Jodie adopts an exaggerated Geordie twang. "Oh hinny, I'm just desperate for a stottie and a Saveloy Dip."

It's Leo's turn to laugh.

"Can we agree," Leo says, "secretly, though that Pease Pudding is fucking rank?"

Jodie gasps in mock horror.

"Sacrilege!" She shouts, pointing at Leo. "Burn the heretic!"

They smile at each other and re-take their seats.

There's a crackle from the Tannoy and a gruff, tired voice spills into the carriage.

"Next stop, Newcastle. Newcastle, next stop."

Outside, through the rain, the countryside has petered out, replaced with long, industrial buildings and yards packed with lines of yellow machinery. This is the last of England's big cities before Scotland. Shipping crates and warehouses whizz past and soon the banks of the Tyne will open like a rift. Leo will be on the last stretch home. His message to mam has finally sent.

The train shudders to a stop at Newcastle. Leo's glad to see that there's only one passenger waiting to get on, a nondescript woman in a beige raincoat.

She clambers aboard, bringing with her the iron smell of cold and sits down in the seat beside the door.

Great, let's go, Leo thinks. He checks his phone; it buzzes to another thumbs up from mam. He hopes that means Chinese takeaway and not a bowl of her soggy bolognese; he'll even offer to walk down to Golden

Orchid in the village and pick it up. The white plastic bag will bounce against his thigh, bulging with cartons of chicken curry in yellow sauce, thick prawn crackers. Leo's mouth is watering.

Just another hour or so on this shitty train and they'll pull into Malacstone where no one but him will get off.

"Good evening to passengers joining us at Newcastle. This is the eight-oh-five service to Ellie Hill calling at…"

Leo sits back into his chair and fumbles in his bag to find his Kindle. He needs to read more books, spend less time on socials, fewer timelapse videos of someone preparing lunch, tanned legs on sun-loungers, everyone else having a generally better time than him.

As Leo unlocks his Kindle and shucks himself further back in his seat to get comfortable, a sudden loud voice makes him jump.

"…yah, fucking nightmare! No, it's fine. I'm on it now. Fucking station's like something out of the Stone Age! Jesus, the North is a fucking dump."

Dah-mp

Leo turns, irritated by the volume of the voice that's burst into his flimsy little sanctuary. The accent.

"Ha! Yeah! The weather up here's like the fucking arctic. At least the beer's cheap and the girls are easy, right?"

Leo feels disgust crawling in his belly.

The owner of the voice is a rosy-cheeked man about Leo's age with curly blonde hair clad in a blue quilted Barbour. He's standing just inside the train door with one of those huge, hiking rucksacks on his back.

"I swear to god, I've got on a fucking tram from the Eighteenth Century or something. Probably have to pay them in whippets." He brays a loud guffaw which turns Jodie's head from across the carriage.

Leo tries to catch her eye. The man is still speaking.

"No, no reserved seats, Jesus *Christ*. First class? You're joking, right."

Clah-s

Leo bristles.

It's not just the man's accent that screams entitlement. There's something in the well-bred hardiness in his muscles and the tan on his skin. That jacket that has never ever seen mud.

The man strides through the carriage, phone clamped to his cheek, bawling into it. Straight backed, confident.

Assured.

The night has never closed down around this guy; he's never felt the bite of emptiness.

He's never had to go without.

"No, I don't know." The man brays more laughter. "Will probably get AIDS from sitting down in this tin-pot train to be honest mate."

This prick goes on skiing holidays and is part of a rowing club and Leo bets he's a student at Durham. 'Roughing it up North'. They're all like this with their rugby shirts and too-loud voices, stomping around like they own the place.

I wonder what this guy's degree is in? Rizz, probably.

"No, if it actually has the fucking capacity for movement." The man is still screaming into his phone. "We should be setting off any moment."

One day, like all the rest of the public school lot, he'll end up being Leo's boss. His dad probably owns Northern Sprinter.

Leo gets that surge of protectiveness for the train again, the end of the county he calls home.

Jesus, the North is a fucking dump.

The man stops next to Leo and looks down his nose. Leo glares. The man looks right back. Unafraid.

Leo, rattled by the confidence of someone who's never been told 'no' before, drops his eyes. Curses his cowardice.

Posho de Twattery walks on, slings his rucksack into the overhead compartment and sits down about equidistant between Leo and Jodie. Leo desperately wants her to look around again. The train doors hiss closed and the engine gathers itself to a start.

"Yeah, setting off now. Nearly missed the fucker!" The man bawls over the rumble of the train. "Couldn't find the bastard platform!"

Leo sighs, a headache already beginning to form in hairline cracks across the front of his skull.

"Yeah, see you later you stupid fucking cunt, yeah? We'll go smash some doors in, all the freshers back in town for Christmas, yeah?"

A peal of braying laughter.

Leo grinds his teeth, tries to radiate his hatred through his eyes and into the back of that stupid curly head.

At least he's finished on his phone now.

The silence in the carriage is vast.

Leo picks up his Kindle.

Beep-beep-boop-boop!

The sound of the notification is maximum volume. Leo looks over to see the guy unlocking his screen and sniggering to himself before replying.

Beep-beep-boop-boop!

Leo drops his head and sighs.

This journey's going to be longer than he could have possibly imagined.

Northumberland National Park
300 Miles North of London

"Can I sit next to you?" Jodie asks.

She's stood in the aisle beside Leo.

Leo nods, shifts closer to the window.

"I'm worried he might come and try to talk to me," she says, voice lowered. "The ick is strong with that one."

Leo pats the seat beside him and Jodie sits down.

The train rattles through the night into the wilderness. The city of Newcastle is long behind them now. Northumberland rolls the train around its vast mouth.

"When I walked past him," Jodie says, staring straight at the plastic seat tray in front of her face, "I heard him say *I'd smash that* to whichever shitbag mate he's talking to. Just loud enough for me to hear."

Leo sighs, shakes his head.

They peer around in their seats. He's still on the phone, one leg lolling in the carriage aisle.

Angus is his name. They both know it because at one point he began bellowing some kind of rugby chant to do with himself drinking and fucking before recounting a story of himself taking a shit in a bin on campus.

Leo and Jodie have had to endure Angus' he-hawing conversation for the last ten minutes.

"No, I dunno mate!" Angus is saying at the top of his voice. "Gonna go watch the Arsenal at the weekend, yeah? You gonna come?"

Leo rolls his eyes and mimes vomiting.

"He's going the wrong way if he wants to do that." Jodie hisses. "Unless Arsenal are playing away?"

"Ok, well, I'll see you there then you, absolute paedophile!" Angus finishes with a peal of laughter.

For a second, they think it's all over.

Beep-beep-boop-boop!

"Heaven help us..." Leo mutters.

"I'd listen to music or something but me fucking headphones are dead," Jodie says.

The Northern Sprinter doesn't have charging points in its seats, as Angus has already loudly informed the entire carriage.

"Fuck," Jodie says. "What a sickener, eh?"

Leo's been trying to read for the last ten minutes but his Alex North book has been stubbornly open on the first page. Angus's voice is eating up the words before they can reach Leo's brain. The rain is hissing against the windows and the train is lurching a little bit back and forth with the wind.

"I was thinking of playing obnoxious TikToks at full volume," Jodie says, glaring at Angus.

"Don't drop to his level," Leo says.

The pair sigh and resume staring out of the window.

Angus phone goes off. A ringtone this time.

Who the fuck even has a ring tone anymore? A chorus of voices recorded in a bar. Some rugby chant. Leo and Jodie look at each other, helpless.

"Hello? Yeah. Not you again, you pillock! What's up?"

Jodie mimes hanging herself. Angus keeps going.

"I swear to God! What the fuck?"

Fah-k

Leo looks over. Angus has taken his jacket off and his tanned elbow points out into the aisle, the phone clasped to the side of his head.

Leo imagines kicking it.

"Bro, I have no idea where I *am* right now!"

At the last stop no one got on or off. The dark has increased, and it feels like another level of cold has begun, seeping through the cracks under the doors. Distant farmhouses pepper the wilds outside. Their lights are snuffed out by the rush of black hills. Leo thinks of the sheep at home, stirring and restless in their straw as the walls of the barn quiver with the weather's rage.

"Hello? *Hello?* God, there you are. No, no. I actually give no shits," Angus bellows with laughter. "I know, right? No, I don't fucking care."

Angus gets to his feet and turns around to face Leo and Jodie.

"How many stops till King's Cross?" he asks.

Angus's voice is the officious blare of someone who'd *like to speak to the manager*.

"King's Cross?" Leo hears Jodie reply. She's hunkered down with her knees up against the seat in front of her.

"Did I stutter?" Angus says.

"I mean, if you're going to London," Leo says, "you're going the scenic way."

Jodie hides a snort of laughter.

Angus' scowl tightens.

"You're fucking joking me," Angus says. "We're going South, right?"

Leo starts to explain to Angus where Northumberland is.

Angus, however, turns to his phone whilst Leo is talking and furiously taps in a number.

"Fuck's sake," Angus says, glaring at his screen. "No bloody signal."

Leo closes his mouth mid-sentence and watches Angus re-take his seat. Jodie stares at him wide-eyed.

"*What-the-fuck?*" she mouths.

Leo shakes his head, can't quite believe that someone can be this rude in real life. He's filled with sudden, righteous anger. He was trying to help. It's not his fault this idiot got the wrong train.

Beep-beep-boop-boop!

Leo grits his teeth; he can hear Angus sighing and muttering.

"Fuck's sake. Fucking North. Fucking shithole."

Beep-beep-boop-boop!

"Finally!" Angus shouts.

Jodie has stopped laughing now. She's glaring in Angus' direction. He's back on the phone.

"Mum?" he says, and his tone is that of someone snapping their fingers at a waiter. "No! No, I'm not! I'm going fucking *north*!"

He gives a huge, withering sigh.

"Mum, come on, engage brain. No, I'm still in the bloody *North* and I'm going *north*. Tu comprends pas?"

Jodie grimaces at Leo.

"If I spoke to my mam like that, I wouldn't be here today!" she says. "Well... I would be, but I wouldn't have any legs!"

Angus is still talking.

"The wrong train. No, the *wrong one*." There's a pause. "*YOU!*" Angus bawls, "Said it would be Platform TWO! No! It was at the last minute. They can't even figure out *platforms* up here and now I'm.... fuck knows where. Some backwood north of Newcastle!"

New-*car-sel*

Leo can't quite believe what he's hearing.

"Hang on," Angus says. He stands up again and walks over.

"Er, *excuse me*." Angus glares down at Leo. "What's the next stop?"

"Underwood," Leo says.

He throws the name at Angus like it's a stone.

"Underwood," Angus repeats. "Right."

He turns from Leo and clamps his phone back to the side of his head. Those sharp edges, the deadly connotations of the name glance off Angus' ignorance and clatter onto the train floor.

"Yeah, mum, some place called Underwood, apparently." Angus begins walking back to his seat.

Leo winces at the name, the incantation. The way Angus has just spat it out loud as if it means nothing.

He's gone to Underwood.

"I DON'T KNOW, SOME fucking sheep-shagging village out in the middle of fuck-knows-where!"

Leo glances over at Jodie, wonders if she feels it too. The atmosphere on the train has changed. Leo has sudden gooseflesh, his lips are peeling back from his teeth.

Stay away from Underwood, Leo love.

Angus, oblivious is still shouting. Leo glares. He sees, in the back of Angus' head, and hears in the whining pitch of his voice, every customer that's been rude to him in the bar; every entitled tosser waving their debit card at him; expectant, like he hadn't realised what he was supposed to be doing standing next to the beer taps and the bottles of spirits.

He sees in Angus, the tall, American woman who marched up to the bar one afternoon and said, 'Espresso Martini?' Arms spread, like it was an accusation.

'I'm sorry, we don't...' Leo started.

She had turned her back on him mid-sentence and went back to her phone.

Leo was nothing to that woman and he's even less to this man.

Leo sighs and turns back to the window as the black land outside undulates past.

Jodie is staring at him, wide-eyed. Leo can see her reflection but can't bring himself to look at her.

"Wow," she says. "Just...wow."

Leo shakes his head. He's so angry, he feels like he might actually cry; a childish knot has begun to form in the back of his throat, and he can feel tears prickling in their ducts. Why has this upset him so much?

He knows why. He turns away from it like that woman in the bar.

"Honestly," Jodie says, nodding at Angus, "I knew people like him exist but I've, like, never seen a specimen in real life."

Leo takes a long, deep breath.

He needs to choose his words carefully. He waits for Angus to be quiet.

At a volume that's just loud enough that Angus can hear him, Leo turns to Jodie.

"Hey, so what do you know about the village of Underwood."

Jodie studies him, brow creased at the sudden volume of his voice.

"Er…"

"Have you ever heard of it before?" Leo says, watching Angus. "Underwood?"

His voice is different, clearer, his vowels broadened, a deepness creeping in. A summoning.

"Have you ever heard of Underwood?"

"I mean," Jodie says and falters. "No? Maybe?"

Jodie looks over at Angus and cottons on; raises her voice slightly. "Oh, you mean *Underwood*? Yeah just, like…it's a ruin, isn't it? A few houses, a pub? It's an old place. An old, old place…"

Leo nods.

"Yes, it is. You're right. Underwood's actually a really interesting place that not many people know about." He nods at Angus. "*Especially* if you're not from here. Like, maybe if you're from down South?"

He's glaring through the headrests at Angus watching every word land.

"Er…right?" Jodie says.

"Underwood," Leo says, nodding toward Angus. "Underwood's one of those places you pass by, just another little station with a tiny platform, a place where no one gets on and no one gets off. At least that's what everyone thinks isn't it? People who aren't from here…"

Leo can hear his mam. He can hear his nanna in his voice now.

"The thing with Underwood," Leo says, "is there's much more to Underwood than people think."

Leo thinks back earlier to the first year on the platform with her trench coat and glasses. *I'm an historian as you know.*

Leo wonders if she's ever heard of Underwood?

"*So,* much more," Jodie says, "to Underwood."

Leo keeps going. All those hours leafing through old books in the library at university only confirmed it: the story there in black and white. His mother's voice. His nanna's warnings. The old story that mam used to tell him, the dark at the windows listening in.

"Of course, everyone from this neck of the woods knows there was once a serious witch-scare in this tiny village. In Underwood."

"There was?" It's Jodie's turn to look over at Angus. He's definitely listening.

"Oh, yes," Leo says. "Witches."

"Are you serious?" Jodie says, looking at Leo. "Like actual witches round here? In Underwood?"

She sounds a little hammy, but Leo doesn't care. So long as Angus can hear them.

Leo takes a breath and waits to see if Angus will look around.

He does.

Leo talks, his voice loud as the night rumbles past. Conjuring up a story that's been burned into his brain since he was a boy.

The Story of Underwood

A blight on the crops; the cattle that weren't giving milk; the two-headed calf that slithered from its dying mother under the light of a bad moon. People whispered about a 'Pale horseman' seen on the hills. A black-cloaked harbinger, of what, no one knew.

A witchfinder, Leo explains, was hired and claimed that Underwood was riddled with daemonic spirits. He advised the village needed to be 'cleansed'.

A magistrate listened to the witchfinder and proclaimed that Underwood was 'infested with an evil that no simple prayers can break' before he ordered the village and its inhabitants, 'all men, women and children that cavort with covetous demons', burnt to the ground.

Underwood was a sore, a boil that needed to be lanced. Anyone who survived the blaze would be 'in league with the devil'.

"So, if you survived a fire, you'd be what?" Jodie says. "Executed? That's quite a flex from the witchfinder."

"Publicly executed," Leo says. "Bro was giving us a vulgar display of power."

"Yeesh," says Angus.

Jodie mouths, *Is that actually true?*

Leo ignores this, goes on talking, taking his time, voice filling the silent carriage as even the train itself seems to curtail its rattling and wheezing as the land begins to rise and the lights of the villages wink out below.

Leo lets the story of Underwood loose from its moorings; riding the howls of the feral wind across the hills. Spilling across the carriages of the Northern Sprinter.

You could see it for miles around, apparently, the flames of Underwood. Like a warning beacon blazing in the darkness. It raged for as long as that mutated calf lived. Afterwards, the smell of burning flesh hung across the hills like fog.

Jodie shivers, "That's grim."

Life was grim in the Seventeenth Century. People needed simple explanations for complex issues.

Switch 'witch' for 'woke' and there's not much difference today.

Leo moves his gaze from Angus' head back out to the darkness outside. There's a break in the rain, the remnants of its lashes cling to the windows. Angus' phone is on his lap. Screen blank. Untouched.

He's still listening.

"The ruins of Underwood are still there," Leo says. "The black stones among the thistles and clumps of grass, a reminder of the mistakes of the past."

"Ugh," Jodie shivers slightly.

The wind has picked up again and is grasping at the rubber round the windows.

Angus leans over to his window and stares out, clamping his hands around his eyes to peer into the blackness.

"Did anyone survive Underwood?" Jodie says.

There's a dip in the engine noise from the train. Expectation.

Something black: a vast, broken tree or a ruined pele tower flashes too close to the window and retreats into the rain.

He never went there, did he? He wouldn't dare.
Police accused of 'giving up hope'.

Leo shivers. He remembers staring out of his bedroom window at night, over the hills, as if one day his father might just come walking back up to the front door, his belongings hanging from a stick over his shoulder and a little dog at his heels.

Leo remembers diving back under his duvet when something moved at the edge of the treeline.

That little version of Leo had been told that there's something worse than witches out there. That's why he's never gone looking for dad.

Maybe the witchfinder was right after all?

Leo shakes his head quickly.

"Only one survived."

The train jolts. Suddenly, Leo and Jodie pitch forward.

The brakes shriek out and the engine shudders to a halt.

A soggy whimper and then nothing.

Still.

"Oh," Jodie says. "Why have we stopped?"

Somewhere in Northumberland National Park Over 300 Miles North of London

Leo can feel the cold creeping into his toes, his fingers, the tip of his nose. It's not going anywhere.

Just like the train.

"It'll be a red light or something, eh?" Jodie says.

Leo nods but this feels like a warning. He hasn't told the last part of the Underwood story.

The train has cut him off.

Leo clears his throat.

"The witchfinder," he says, doing everything to rough-ride over a stammer, "who condemned Underwood, vanished the next day."

"What?" Jodie's got her phone out, waving it above her head. The screen is defiantly blank.

Leo's mouth is dry, and they both jump as the train lets out a sudden hiss. Just the brakes, Leo tells himself, just something letting out pressure because of the emergency stop.

That's all. That's *all*.

"They found his carriage," Leo says, "Abandoned on the road leading down from the hills. No horse, no driver. No one inside."

There's another hiss, a clunk from the bowels of the train.

The warm air that was pumping from the vents has stopped. Only the howl of the wind sounds from outside. Mournful and ragged.

"For fuck's sake…" Angus' irritated whisper blunts the fear, muffles the magic.

Leo's grateful for it. He should never have told this story in the first place.

He turns to Jodie but can't think of what to say; an uncertainty creeps into the carriage like the freezing air. Jodie pulls her hat back on and snuggles into her scarf. She avoids his eye.

He hopes to fuck the train hasn't broken down.

"Shouldn't have mentioned Underwood," Jodie sing-songs and Leo very nearly tells her to shut up.

Movement up ahead. Leo, Jodie and Angus all crane their necks to see the door to their carriage stutter open and a woman in a beige raincoat shuffling through. She's stooped and wears a knitted black hat. Her breath comes in puffs of condensation as she stares around at the three of them.

"Eeh," she says in a thick Scouse accent. "It's no better in here, is it? Bloody freezing."

Leo feels obliged to respond and he gives her a big smile to try and juxtapose Angus' glare. The woman shuffles closer along the carriage grasping the headrests of each seat, beaming at Leo.

"You young 'uns'll be alright, won't you?" she says. "Don't feel the cold like us older girls."

She chuckles and Leo feels himself relaxing slightly.

"I know," the woman says. "I'm sorry, I'm not a looney tune. I just came to see if it was any warmer in this carriage. If any of youse knew what was going on?"

Jodie unwinds her scarf from her face and smiles up at the woman.

"Are you warm enough?" Jodie says and holds up the scarf. Cable knitted. Swamp green. "Do you want to borrow this?"

"Don't be daft!" The woman says, waving her hand. "I'm a tough old bird! You're alright love. Thanks, though."

Jodie grins. Leo can see Angus mouthing out her words, his face twisted up in a grin, mimicking her accent.

"Always happens here, though," the woman says. "Doesn't it?"

There's a pause.

Does it?

Leo looks at Jodie who shrugs. The woman turns to Leo.

"Sorry," Leo says. "I get this train a lot and it's never…"

He peters out.

Angus is scowling down at his phone, tapping at his screen with a single finger like a heron snatching at the surface of a pond.

"I know I don't sound like I'm from round here," the woman says, smiling. "But I come this way a lot, too."

"You don't sound like you're from this country, love."

If the woman heard Angus, she doesn't acknowledge him.

She keeps going.

"I know about all the weird stuff in this neck of the woods." She gives a laugh, a cackling that jars in the frozen silence of the train. "The Hexham Heads, the Bamburgh Beast. Nothing quite like Underwood though is there?"

"Really?" says Jodie.

"That's right round here," the woman nods and points out the window. "Round Underwood. There's something not quite right."

Breath catches in Leo's throat. A sudden weight in his chest.

Please don't...

"Looney tune," Angus says, louder this time and the smile slides from the woman's face.

Her brow furrows. She turns to face Angus who pretends to be concentrating very hard on his phone.

"There's no point," the woman says, pointing at Angus.

"What?" he says, testily.

"The phone. You divvy." The woman mimics Angus' incessant tapping.

Jodie snorts with laughter. Angus' face is scarlet. The woman jabs her finger at him. "There's no signal for your silly little device. Not round Underwood. Never has been, never will be."

Angus sighs and pushes his phone into his pocket.

"I mean," he says, "that's more to do with the fact that we're in the middle of nowhere actually. It's got nothing to do with *witches*."

There is a pause. The woman in the beige coat does smile now, unperturbed.

"Who said anything about witches, lad?"

Ha, Leo thinks, looking at Angus, *clamped*.

Angus gives a snort.

"There's no witches round here," she says, shaking her head. "Not anymore."

Leo feels a chill creep over his skin, gooseflesh rising on his arms. It's the cold, he thinks, the frozen air outside.

Jodie's leg presses gently into his. She feels it, too.

Angus breaks the silence.

"We could do with a spell to get us moving again…" he says. It's an attempt at humour. The woman doesn't take it.

Good, Leo thinks.

"You know what they say about lads like you round here?" she says.

The woman waits, her eyes boring into Angus. He can't ignore her. He twists in his seat.

"What?" says Angus, at last. Petulant, sulky.

"They say that the Gangral will come for you."

The word lands and Leo feels it. Those syllables that have cavorted in his nightmares since he was a kid.

Gangral.

She jabs one pointed finger at Angus who looks up and widens his eyes in mock horror.

"The Gangral always comes for naughty little boys like you."

Leo wants to close his eyes and curl into a ball until this is over.

"Sure," Angus says, his tone flat, bored. "Whatever you say."

The woman turns back to Leo and Jodie.

"Youse two know the Gangral, don't you?" she says. "Everyone round here knows about the Gangral."

Leo opens his mouth but Jodie cuts in.

"Gangral?" she says. "That's an old Northumbrian word, isn't it? Not gangrel with an 'e' but *Gangral*. A noun rather than an adjective, right?"

There you go, Leo thinks, *your linguistic knowledge has finally had its use in the real world.*

The woman in the beige coat clicks her fingers with a dusty *snap*. She points at Jodie.

"That's right," she says. "It is. Gangral. A noun. A name. Smart girl."

"It means, like, a vagrant, or a wanderer, right? Something like that?" Jodie says. "From the verb *gan*?"

Angus cuts in.

"You mean a bin-dipper. A tramp?" He wears a smirk.

"Wind your neck in," the woman says to him. "I'm trying to talk to these two here. No one asked for your opinion."

"Free speech," Angus says. "I'm allowed to have an opinion you know."

"Course you are," the woman says, "and so am I. My opinion is that you're a nasty, entitled little boy."

Angus drops his head.

"Ooof." Leo is grinning. Jodie mimes a mic-drop.

"Call an ambulance," Jodie whispers. "I think there's just been a murder."

There's a sudden jolt and rumble. The woman pitches forward and grabs on to the nearest seat. Leo feels his heart flutter to the back of his throat and sink slowly back into place. The train has begun moving again.

"There we go," the woman says. "Off we pop, see you later, you two. I'm going back to me seat." And she turns and shuffles away. Angus pretends to be engrossed with his phone but he's blushing.

Leo turns to Jodie and opens his mouth to speak.

Beep-beep-boop-boop!

He sighs instead.

"Not so clever now are you," comes Angus's voice from up ahead. Then he speaks even lower, "You old twat."

Fucking coward, Leo thinks. *I hope the Gangral comes for you.*

Somewhere in Northumberland
Many Miles North of London

The Gangral.

This is the word that Leo had no intention whatsoever of saying; the weapon he would always keep sheathed.

But now the final part of the Underwood story, the one he wasn't going to tell has stepped onto the train and announced itself. An unwanted guest.

As soon as Leo heard the word, *Gangral*, he was a kid again and those two syllables crouched at the edge of night, waiting for mam to turn off his bedside light.

That word clatters along with the rattle of the train.

Gan-gral, gan-gral, gan-gral.

Jodie's fallen asleep, her hat pulled down over her eyes. Her breath is coming in little rumbles from her half-open mouth. Leo presses his forehead onto the cold of the window, letting it vibrate through his skull as he watches the darkness go by.

Gan-gral, gan-gral, gan-gral.

With every hill and tree and field that whizzes past, he's closer to home. Closer to those whispered childhood stories.

Gan-gral, gan-gral, gan-gral.

He's trying not to let his fears in, the ones that run alongside the train. Tricks of the shadows outside.

What does the Gangral look like, mam?

The smell of his mam: waxy lanolin and talcum powder. Her calloused hands, rough like chicken feet. The farm work she took on after dad vanished tightened her muscles. Stretched her sinews. Made her tough.

Tougher.

The only people who know that, Leo, are the ones what don't come back...

Like dad?

A lop-sided grin. The smoke of the roll-up in the corner of her mouth. Grey hair escaping from her hat.

Leo had grinned back. He was strong. A big boy. Leo wishes he felt like a big boy now as he stares out into the gloom. There's nothing out there, darker than the night. There never was anything out there, he thinks.

No pale rider. No Gangral.

No dad wading through the hillside like a ragged spectre.

Leo pulls away from the dancing darkness, the rain playing tricks on him. He pulls out his Kindle again, but the words won't behave.

The Gangral Gangral

By Alex Gangral

There's movement and Leo watches Angus pull himself to his feet and wander off down the carriage, phone clasped to the side of his face. His rucksack is still stuffed into the overhead compartment, a single frayed strap dangling just above head height. Angus passes through the automatic doors between the carriages and vanishes.

The plastic WC sign above the carriage door does not illuminate; Angus is not in the toilet.

Beep-beep-boop-boop!

Jodie stirs but does not wake. Leo turns to follow the sound, confused.

The noise of the alert is coming from Angus' seat but Leo saw him holding his phone when he left. Why does he have two phones?

Is there more to Angus than they thought?

Leo's tempted to go over there, steal this other phone and throw it out the window but that would make him the bad guy in all this and Leo's way too stubborn to do that.

Beep-beep-boop-boop!

Annoying, but it's better than his own brain whispering memories at him right now

The train has slowed, limping through the night and the rain does not relent. All around them are thick trees and finally Leo recognises where they are.

Gan-gral, gan-gral, gan-gral.

There's a muted *thwack* sound from the other side of the train as wet leaves and branches lap at the windows like hungry, green tongues.

He has no idea what this woodland is called but it's one of the beacons that signals the way home. The branches scratch at the side of the train windows, clattering like bones. It's not going to be long before they get to Underwood. Then it's only Darkton and Colliwell before Malacstone; mam and Chinese takeaway. Darkton's just another stop. A little village where no one gets on or off. Colliwell has a Thai restaurant built into the station and from the train window, you can see people tucking happily into sticky rice and Pad Thai.

Leo's stomach gives a gurgle and it's so loud that Jodie shifts in her slumber beside him.

Leo apologises as she wakes, eyes opening slowly, cat-like. He's been bursting for a piss for a while now and this seems like an opportune moment.

Jodie tucks her knees up to her chin and Leo gets up. He walks down the aisle of the carriage, holding onto the headrests of the other seats as the train lurches and the branches thwack more urgently at the windows.

Leo lingers at the empty seat where Angus has just been. There's his coat and a discarded coffee cup. There's also a book which surprises Leo. It's some kind of Make Yourself AWESOME self-help title and it doesn't look like it's ever been opened.

No phone though.

Worried in case Angus reappears, Leo keeps moving until he reaches the automatic door at the end of the carriage which puffs open. It's noisy in the vestibule which smells of diesel mixed with the acrid reek of chemicals from the toilet. The door closes behind him and he's in that liminal, shaky space with the carriage couplings only a couple of feet beneath his own.

Rails and rocks and rust.

The rain and the wind mix with the rattle of the train's wheels on the tracks and the panting engine. Leo doesn't like how close outside feels, it's only a little bit of metal that's between him and the darkness.

Between him and *the Gangral*.

Stop it.

Leo faces the toilet door. He's gearing up to hold his breath and press the entry button. He hopes to get things done as quickly as possible without touching a single surface and get out of there but a sound distracts him.

A voice.

Leo holds his breath. The voice is just above a whisper and there's a furrow of sorrow coursing through it. Leo turns away from the toilet and cranes his neck.

There's someone standing on the other side of the vestibule, not six feet from him, crouched into where the carriage door is. Their back to him. They're talking in hushed sobs into their phone.

It's Angus.

Leo exhales as quietly as he can and listens.

"No mummm...." A child-like whine and then Angus says, "I *can't*...I don't know who to ask..."

Leo feels a grin spreading across his face. He turns back to his carriage to see if he can alert Jodie somehow, but he can't see her from here. He takes out his phone and unlocks the camera, switching to video. The train sways and Leo pitches slightly to one side, praying Angus doesn't look around. Jodie's going to love this too.

"I don't even know where I *am*...." Angus is sobbing. "It's horrible up here...there's just nothingness for miles and miles and…and…" Now he does begin to cry. "And…It feels like…like… there's *something out there…*"

The train rattles and shakes. Leo plants his feet. He can't believe his luck. His own childhood terrors start to evaporate in the wake of Angus' mewling. His thumb hovers over 'record'.

"Mum…I'm scared…" Angus says. "I'm really fucking scared…"

Then he dissolves into tears. Leo expects laughter to come but it doesn't. Instead, Leo, in Angus' voice, hears the scared little boy that he used to be. With a moment of clarity, Leo suddenly understands all the bluster, the shouting, the arrogance. It's a mask, a show, it's there to hide Angus' fear.

Leo's mirth is replaced by hot shame.

It's the same way Leo stands on train platforms, judging precocious freshers and glaring at people from behind the bar on campus. His own mask of sarcastic bitterness disguises a similarly scared little boy who's still waiting for his dad to come home.

Leo thinks of his mam; how she towered over him when he was little. His hero. There was always a fight going on between her heart and her head playing out on her face. Her hands on his shoulders. Her voice.

She showed him how to be strong.

She showed him how strong she was, facing the aching empty space in her bed.

Dad's muddy Barbour jacket on the hook in the hall.

He's gone to Underwood.

Young Leo had made a silent promise that he wouldn't be scared. How he wouldn't run.

This isn't strength.

Leo remembers pushing past younger kids, fist already chambered after Keith Burn had sung *Chirpy-Chirpy Cheep-Cheep* in the dinner queue and replaced 'mama' with 'daddy'. A little ooh followed his progress over the scrape of plastic trays.

Everything had gone red and throbbing like the inside of a wound. Leo's second knuckle still stubbornly sits out of place.

Pain numbs.

Angus takes a great, trembling breath and pulls himself together. Leo stares down at his own feet.

"Ok, mum. I will." Angus voice still carries the echo of a little boy. "Next station, yeah? I'll get off. There'll be someone I can ask. Or an Uber to a hotel, yeah? Ok, I'll let you know how much it is."

Angus sniffles.

"Thanks, mum."

Leo turns his camera off and feels a bit of a twat. He's judged Angus just like he feels Angus has judged him, Jodie and the woman in the beige coat. He's no better. He judged Angus as Angus has judged the North.

Leo's spent most of his life moaning about Malacstone; its inward nature, the fact everyone knows everyone. He resents that his friends are low-key upset with him for leaving and actually trying to make something of himself.

We're all just lost sheep, Leo thinks. *Crying out for our mammy's amid the bleak hills of fucking nowhere.*

Angus can't help where he's from any less that Leo can.

Leo imagines himself being lost in the South. On the tube perhaps? Or in one of those bleak commuter cities, night falling around the endless alleyways and identikit buildings.

He has felt the same as Angus probably does now on the odd occasions when Leo has had to go to London. A gig. A convention. The vastness of the place overwhelms him. Coach-loads of tourists being swallowed slowly; the city is a bloated python, scales smeared with oil and grease. Leo has stared up at mould-flecked windows in tower blocks, concrete darkness under stairwells. Endless rows of lonely decrepitude. The belly of the beast. It's a place to be utterly forgotten.

To be lost.

Leo decides there and then that he'll drop all his prejudice. He'll help Angus. But after he's been for a piss.

Leo stands in the train toilet under a baleful yellow light. As he's pissing, he decides he's not going to tell Jodie about Angus' moment of vulnerability. Leo can't forget the tone of his voice, that little-boy sound; it reminds him of being a kid again, peering through the gap in the curtain over the night-cloaked hills of home. The story of the Gangral creeping into every thought.

There's a crackle of feedback from the Tannoy and Leo spatters one trouser leg.

"Fuck's sake."

"Underwood next stop. Next stop, Underwood."

Here we are, Leo thinks. *The inevitability of the place.*

Leo finishes up and steps out of the toilet hoping that the smell of it hasn't clung to his clothes and the stains on his jeans aren't too obvious.

The train is grinding to a halt and Leo can see Angus, red faced and surly, coat on, heaving his bag from the overhead compartment. Leo advances into the carriage.

He wants to say something, wants to impart some kind of sympathy. *I know how you feel, my guy. I know what it's like to feel lost.*

He also wants to tell Angus not to get out here.

Stay away from Underwood.

"Um..." Leo starts. "Are you ok?"

Angus turns to him and their eyes meet.

Leo opens his mouth, not quite knowing what he's going to say next.

Beep-beep-boop-boop!

Leo grits his teeth. Some of that sympathy evaporates as Angus turns to his phone.

Underwood is just a place. Angus is just some guy.

The train stops. A single lamp that lights Underwood's tiny platform.

No one stands on the platform. The concrete glitters in the cold. A thousand little eyes.

Angus shoulders his rucksack, walks out of the train carriage and onto the platform without a word. His feet make no sound.

He's gone to Underwood.

Behind him the door hisses closed. He doesn't look back.

Leo takes his seat next to Jodie, sighing, and the two of them watch as the train pulls away. Angus' face is illuminated by the glow of distant, orange streetlamp, watching the train leave. He and Underwood are eventually swallowed by the darkness.

North of Underwood
Over 350 Miles North of London

"I wonder if there even *is* a train south?" Jodie says, looking at her phone. "At this time, I mean?"

Leo shrugs. Now that Angus is gone, the carriage is quiet again save for the rumble of the train's engine. Leo stares out of the window; they're long past Underwood, having picked up a bit of speed. The name of the Gangral is fading away too.

Leo stares out at the hills as the rain hammers down in great lashes. He can't stop thinking about Angus, all alone out there on his own. His tears still echoing softly through the chambers of Leo's mind.

"You ok?" Jodie says, looking at him.

"Just knackered. Want to get home."

Leo's tempted to text mam and see if she wants to meet him at Colliwell. Maybe eat some Thai. Then he thinks better of it.

Face to face over a green curry, there'll be no escape. She'll ask him what he's going to do *after* his master's. She'll say there's no *career progression* in bar work. As if he doesn't know. All the little micro-aggressions that he escaped from at uni will start crawling under his skin. Best just to get home, eat some bolognese and go up to his room.

He hopes Angus manages to get in touch with his own mam.

"Do you think he got out there on purpose?" Jodie says, suddenly.

Leo asks her what she means.

"Underwood, you know, after he heard us talking about it?"

Leo shrugs.

"I wonder if he was trying to look tough," Jodie goes on. "I mean, bro's going to end up sleeping on a bench in the station. Good luck getting a taxi, let alone a hotel round there, my guy."

Leo holds back a shiver.

He's only ever passed through Underwood. Never stopped.

He was little, riding up top with mam in the truck pulling the trailer full of sheep along the winding roads. Jip, their Collie, sat like a good girl on the flatbed, tongue out, wind in her face watching the emptiness go by.

Leo remembers not liking the place then; a swarthy little village in the midst of a boggy marshland. Underwood was full of locked doors, homemade, 'Private Property. Keep Out' signs in black paint; walls topped with broken glass and rusted barbed wire. There was a pub he hoped mam didn't want to visit. A man with a bull-like face stood, smoking on the front step. Leo remembers the tension in his mam's back. How her face tightened.

He remembered looking out for dad and not telling her. Making sure she couldn't see it in his face. But his eyes scanned every moss-ridden roof, every broken pavement.

Leo remembers being scared, wondering if dad would just be *there*, around the next corner pruning a hedge, stroking a cat. Leo would call out and dad might look up, his eyes blank, face confused.

Who are you, kid? Like something out of a dream.

As if Underwood itself had snatched dad and refused to give him back.

A petulant child who wouldn't share their toys.

Leo likes to think he's seen those black stones on the hill, the remnants of the burned village but maybe that's just in his head?

"Can I tell you something?" Jodie says and Leo pulls away from the window and looks at her.

"I've not actually ever heard of the Gangral."

"Really?" Leo is surprised. "You grew up south of the Tyne though. Maybe it's a Northumberland thing that only us sheep farmers know about?"

Jodie shrugs.

"Maybe? I've not heard my missus talk about it either and she's more Northern than you!"

"She's practically a wildling if she lives up in Ellie Hill," Leo says and Jodie grins.

"That lot are the reason Hadrian built his wall!"

They both laugh.

Leo looks at the window again; Underwood station is far enough behind them. The end of the story has been crouched taught like a predator waiting to spring.

He might as well let it out.

He tells Jodie in the same way mam told him; adopting her intonation she only used for telling stories; the way her eyes searched the horizon.

When Underwood was burned, mam said, only two single souls survived the blaze. A child and his mother. They ran from their burning home, pursued by the witchfinder's dogs. The little lad crawled through the marsh and hid in the mud and the reeds as the stink of scorched flesh billowed behind him on clouds of black smoke.

Jodie's turn to shiver.

"What about the mam?"

Leo remembers asking his mam the same thing, his stomach fizzing with worry.

"Back then, they used Irish Wolfhounds as hunting dogs." Mam had told him and he'd looked at a picture of them in a book in the corner of Malacstone library one afternoon. Great grey things with shaggy hair. Troll-dogs, he thought back then. Wild eyed and wiry with lolling tongues.

In mam's story, the boy waited until nightfall before fleeing south, crawling through the marsh, slathering himself in mud so those troll-dogs couldn't catch his scent. When he emerged on the road, he stood trembling before a pale horseman who had descended from the hill, silent as a prayer.

The moon lit the horseman like a spotlight.

"I assume that horseman is the devil, right?" Jodie says.

Leo presumes so too; a lot of folk stories depict Old Nick as a rider on a lonely road. Meeting him is never a good idea.

"The rider tells the child he can bring him to his mother in exchange for his mortal soul."

"Naturally."

"But the kid's smart; he's caked in mud from head to toe, the rushes and reeds hanging from him."

Like a new skin.

There is something about that description that haunted Leo, rearing up from childhood and reaching for him in the dark. Leo, tucked up with his Ben 10 duvet and the soft yellow of his bedside lamp, couldn't comprehend such inhumanity.

The boy tells the devil, no deal, and the devil curses the boy. He'll wander the hills forever, a creature of mud and moss, a pelt of reeds, a hollow in his heart and a hunger in his belly. Always searching for his mother.

Always searching for a meal.

Always searching for home.

His teeth would grow like the tusks of some wild thing, and he would forego the trappings of man.

"Jesus, that's awful," Jodie says.

The boy staggers from village to village, banging on doors and calling out for his mother. His mouth a bloody hole, his voice rasping like the cry of a beast. People think he's some kind of demon and he's shunned wherever he goes. As time goes by, the boy becomes less human, more...

"Feral?" Jodie says and Leo nods.

"They say the Gangral still haunts the hills around Underwood. Still searching for his mother. If you feel his hand in yours on some lonely road, he'll take you."

The train rumbles on and the rain does not relent. Leo feels a little bit guilty, and he opens his mouth to cover the story he's unleashed with a joke when a noise pierces the air making them both jump.

Beep-beep-boop-boop!

Leo and Jodie stare at each other. Surely not.

"Let me." Jodie leaps up from her seat and sets off down the carriage, scanning the seats. Leo can't believe it. No one just forgets their phone, do they? Maybe Angus was so frazzled, so scared, that it slipped his mind. But didn't he have two phones? He seemed the type.

"Which one was his seat again?"

Beep-beep-boop-boop!

Leo points vaguely to the middle of the carriage but he's confused, the sound of the phone seems further away now. As if it's moved. Jodie's casting around in frustration.

"I can't see it. Do you think..."

The train jolts and Jodie pitches forward. Leo gets up now and she pulls herself into one of the seats as Leo passes her in the aisle.

It'll be in the vestibule. That's where he must have left it.

"Poor fucker," Jodie says "Imagine leaving your phone."

Leo reaches the end of the carriage. The door slides open, and he peers around the corner to where Angus was sitting, sobbing at his mother.

"Nothing here," Leo calls back, "Keep looking!"

He stares at the empty space beside the door where Angus sat. The engine rattles and roars as the train ascends further North.

"I can't see one here," Jodie shouts from the carriage.

A shudder passes through the growl of the engine noise. Another jolt.

The train is losing speed again. The brakes shriek and Leo clings on to the wall next to the toilet door. The scream of the breaks increases its pitch and the train grinds to a rattling halt.

Not again.

Leo walks back into the carriage, stopping the automatic door with one foot before it closes on him.

"Are we at Colliwell already?" he says but he knows fine well that they're not.

This motion is too quick, too urgent. There's no Thai restaurant here in the dark. No streetlamps, no stations.

Only darkness.

There's been no announcement either. Just the endless tattoo of the rain.

Leo tries in vain to stop a sinking feeling in his belly.

This is worse than before.

Jodie is standing, eyes wide, looking at the ceiling of the train, waiting for an announcement.

Please, Leo thinks. *Please just say we'll be moving soon.*

...in exchange for my mortal soul

Leo tells his brain to shut the fuck up with that sort of nonsense.

"Ah, shit," Jodie says. "Must be the weather."

Leo disagrees. It can't be. It's not *that* bad is it? He peers out of the nearest window. The land is flat around here; long stretches of ragged fields, marshes where rickety fences poke out occasionally like the rigging of some sunken vessel. A few twisted trees are buffeted back and forth by the wind.

(DON'T) CALL MUM 77

When the crackle across the Tannoy comes, Leo feels his whole body sag with relief. We'll be moving again soon. Just a red light. Just one of those inexplicable train stops. He doesn't care.

The announcement is quick and mumbled.

"Could Mr. Black contact a member of train staff please. Mr. Black, thank you."

Leo looks at Jodie who shrugs.

"Let's hope Mr. Black is some kind of train technician, eh?"

Leo can't shake a terrible, squirming notion clinging to him that something is wrong. He walks through the still carriage, holding onto the headrests and swinging himself back into his seat. Jodie joins him. A draught is creeping in from outside and the carriage rocks slightly with the roar of the wind.

The rain does not relent.

"You don't think," Jodie says, eventually.

Leo looks around.

"I mean…Angus. Maybe he realised he didn't have his phone and somehow, I dunno, managed to get the train stopped?"

"They wouldn't stop a train," Leo says, "for a phone, would they?"

They fall back into an uncertain silence that yawns between them.

"Um," Jodie says, "I don't want to worry you or anything..."

Leo looks at her, suddenly uncertain.

"Like, it might be important," Jodie says, then drops her voice slightly, "but I used to work in a theatre part-time, selling ice creams and that. When we started, we had this training day where you had to learn all the emergency codes."

Leo doesn't like the sound of this.

"So, obviously," Jodie goes on, "when some shit goes down, they don't want mass panic so the announcements across the Tannoy that you hear are usually codes for something else."

Leo's trying not to look out of the window because he's sure that something moved.

Just a tree, just the wind.

"For example," Jodie says, "in our theatre at least, if you heard, *could the driver of the silver Ford Anglia please contact reception.* It meant that there was trouble in the bar.

"What happened if there actually was a silver Ford Anglia in the car park?"

Jodie shrugs.

"I dunno. It never happened."

There's the movement again in the corner of Leo's eye; it must just be a reflection in the window of his and Jodie's distorted doppelgängers hunched in the seats. Jodie's hand. Leo's imagination. But a slithering feeling in Leo's stomach says otherwise. Something is moving outside. Something is dragging itself through the rain toward the train.

Leo turns in his seat to face Jodie. His back to the window.

"Um...ok..." she says. "Anyway, one of the codes was *Would Mr. Groves please contact the front desk.*"

Leo asks what that meant, or does he actually want to know? Jodie wets her lips.

"It meant there was a suspected bomb on the premises."

Leo lets out his breath in a long whistle.

"I never heard that one used either," Jodie says, "but when I heard Mr. Black just then on here it just sounded..."

Ominous.

Leo doesn't know what to say.

"Hang on!" Jodie suddenly shouts, making Leo jump. "What if that Angus guy is Mr. Black?"

Leo is confused.

"Hear me out. Like, what if Angus called his mam and then she's been trying to get in touch with him because he lost his phone?"

Jodie's eyes are full of hope and Leo doesn't want to dash it. It's better than a bomb.

The phone, Leo thinks. *We never actually found it.*

"Come on," Leo says, and they both get to their feet again, sweeping up and down the carriage to try and find the errant device. It might have fallen under a seat.

"I'm going to check in the overhead thing," Jodie says, clambering onto one of the seats.

Leo is glad of the distraction and squats down, peering under the rows of static chairs. He keeps his gaze averted from the windows where night peers in at them. Nothing. Leo unlocks his own phone and turns on the torch, sweeping a ray of light into the dark. He winces slightly; the grooves of the rubber floor filled with years of the contents of people's shoes.

Beep-beep-boop-boop!

Leo's thigh collides with an armrest. His leg deadens immediately. He groans and staggers.

"Are you ok?" Jodie says.

"Fine but where is that coming from?"

They both stare around.

"It *has* to be here," Jodie says. "It must have fallen between."

But whatever Jodie thinks is forgotten instantly as something slams with a terrible meaty thud against one of the windows.

Leo cries out and topples over, the pain in his leg forgotten. Jodie shrieks. As Leo falls hard against an unrelenting seat, the musty reek of it, diesel and unwashed hair, comes up to meet him. The corner of his eye catches movement against the window, some blurry figure, darker than the night.

Two pale eyes.

"Jesus fuck, Jesus fuck...what the fuck was that?" Jodie says, her voice wavering.

Mr. Black.

Leo's mouth is dry and he can't even form words. He crouches half in and half out of the train seat, not daring to look up, wanting to curl into a little ball instead, close his eyes until this hellish journey is over.

"*Is it gone?*" Leo is disgusted at the piteous terror in his voice. He's a little boy again woken up in the darkness of not quite morning, reality and a nightmare dancing a terrible tango outside his bedroom window. His father is gone, his coat still hanging like a shroud from the peg in the hall.

Leo wants his mam to come and save him. The shadow of his father is behind her. His face blurred out.

"I think it's gone," Jodie says. "It was only there for a second...fuck."

Leo unfolds himself, daring to look at where the sound came from.

One of the train windows, a few seats down from theirs, has a mark on it; a stain as if wet soil was slopped against it from the outside. Leo inches closer to Jodie and wishes she would hold onto him, so he doesn't have to be the one to hold onto her.

"What in the name of God was that?" Leo says.

There's a smudge in the mud on the window – the shapes of two splayed hands.

That can't be possible.

"Bird strike," Jodie says in a breathy little whisper. "Look." She points at the stain. The handprints and Leo forces his brain to turn them into wings.

"Yeah," Leo says. "Bird strike...that's all. Two of them."

They stare out into the blackness, Leo praying that there's not something out there, prowling, circling the train.

The only sound is the lowing of the wind and the rain coming in wave after wave.

Bird strike. That's all.

Leo forces himself to think of tiny bones shattering against glass and the feverish flutter of a broken wing.

That's what any movement outside will be. A poor injured bird, confused by the weather, uncomprehending of the train.

He doesn't think about a loping black shape rearing out of the tree line in the distance. Two paw-like palms against the window, caked in marsh-filth.

"Poor thing," Jodie says in a half-hearted murmur still staring out the window.

Leo doesn't know what else to say. The night glares in from all sides.

Something shimmers in the rain and Leo can hear a faint keening coming from his own chest.

There's something standing in the dark, a few feet away, something humanoid, a terrible ragged shadow.

"What the fuck?" Leo begins to point, and a whirling starts in his belly.

"What?" Jodie says, suddenly urgent. "What?"

But there's a grunt and a rumble and a jolt, the train begins to move again. The engine reverberates and the shape is gone.

Leo breathes out and turns away from the window.

"Nothing," he says. "There's nothing there."

Beep-beep-boop-boop!

Leo is almost glad for the distraction. He bends to the floor again, so dedicated to his search for the phone, he won't have to look at the windows. He's happy to do this until they reach Malacstone and he can get out and call mam.

A crackle from the Tannoy.

"Next stop is Darkton. Darkton, next stop."

Leo's sleeve is filthy from reaching under the seats. Blue spiderwebby dust clings to him, and Jodie gags slightly when he turns to her.

"Jesus, that's grim," she says, getting to her feet.

Leo goes to smell his sleeve then thinks better of it. So far he's found a couple of pound coins amid the filth and twists of old chewing gum, hard and puckered.

Anything's better than thinking about those hands. Those eyes.

Leo's going to go and wash, clean his sleeve, soak it in that gloopy pink soap that strains from the grimy dispenser in the toilet.

"That's the last bit of the carriage to search and if it's not anywhere under there," Jodie says, pointing at the top corner where four seats crowd around a blue plastic table patterned with circular coffee stains, "we're both hearing things and have lost our minds."

Leo nods. Mouth dry.

The village of Darkton approaches.

The train has begun to slow. Leo chances a glance at the window and to his relief a few lights peer between the mess of mud. He watches welcome rows of decrepit miners' cottages stagger past on the other side. At last, they're out of the dark.

Darkton, is another stop on the way home, another place to leave. An empty street where a pothole brims with water; a back garden with muddy plastic toys and a sodden rabbit shivering in the corner of a hutch. But it's better than nothing right now.

The train heaves itself to a stop, brakes squealing.

"This is Darkton," says the voice from the Tannoy.

Leo feels a weight shift, his fear diminish.

Neither Leo nor Jodie have discussed with each other what they're going to do with Angus' phone when they find it, but it's come as such a welcome distraction that they speak of nothing else. Not Mr. Black nor the Gangral. If they find it the second before the train pulls up at Malacstone, all will be perfect. Leo's tempted to keep it; sell it perhaps. He thinks of Angus alone on the platform at Underwood and he can't help feeling bad.

"He'll be ok, won't he?" Leo says out loud and Jodie shrugs.

"Yeah, I mean, yeah. He might get cold but it's not like he's stuck in the Outback, is he? Underwood's got houses, a pub. Plus he's a man. I don't think either of us would have let a lone woman who didn't know where she was get off at Underwood, right?"

Stay away from Underwood, Leo love.

"Right." Leo likes to think he wouldn't. Tells himself he wouldn't.

There is a hiss, a robotic gasp and the carriage door opens.

Someone is getting onboard.

Leo cranes his neck as the cold slithers in through the open door; uncertainty in his stomach like some vast hand rises up from dark waters, dripping with filth and pondweed.

"Who's...oh..." Jodie's voice is cut short.

A figure steps inside the train from the platform with a grunt, carrying the reek of rain and cold with an undercurrent of something clean, cologne or deodorant or shampoo.

Leo tries to speak but his mouth has seized up. His tongue withers and dies and his expression slackens. The hulking figure who has entered the train glances his way with eyes that hold no recognition.

Leo's mouth finally opens, his lips peeling from each other, his mouth making an empty *paaaa* sound as if trying to form a word before engaging his brain.

But the person, the passenger has already turned from Leo and pulls the bulky hiking rucksack off their back. They wear a blue quilted Barbour jacket that has never seen a field. Angus pushes his rucksack onto the baggage rack and swings himself into a seat without a word.

Darkton, Northumberland
Miles and Miles and Miles North of London

LEO AND JODIE HAVE agreed in whispers that *yes, it's him*. It's Angus. There's no mistake. The pair take it in turns to half-stand and peer through the gap in the headrests at the man a few seats in front of them.

"He's got a phone," Jodie says, sitting down and staring at Leo.

Leo swallows, not sure what this all means. The train door closes, and the engine picks up. They depart from Darkton and the lights of the village fade.

The train rattles on into the night.

The phone that Leo and Jodie can't find has not made a sound since this other Angus re-joined the train.

Leo doesn't know what to say. He's trying to think of all the ways that Angus could have made it from Underwood to Darkton this fast.

He goes back again to the winding roads of his childhood: mam staring, roll-up clenched between her lips. Her knuckles, pale as she manoeuvres through the winding roads.

Those journeys seemed to take hours and hours.

Sometimes they would see the train. It was a train like this one, plunging into trees and below the swell of the hills.

But maybe his childhood memories have distorted the time. Maybe it's easy to get between Underwood and Darkton now?

"It's not impossible," Leo eventually says. "He'd have to have had a taxi literally waiting at Underwood and then it would have had to have gone hell for leather over the hills to get to Darkton and even then…"

He trails off and wishes Jodie would stop looking at him for an answer. He can't offer her anything.

He turns to the window, staring out at the night.

In the reflection, he can see Angus, this strange new Angus, sitting in a seat. The guy has the same languid arrogance as before, one foot lolling into the aisle; Nike crew socks pulled over his ankles; downy hair on tanned skin as his trouser leg rides up.

Maybe it isn't Angus. Maybe it's just one of those freakish coincidences and this guy just looks like him?

"He seems…fine," Jodie whispers. "Like, he's not screaming into his phone this time."

In fact, since he got on again, this Angus has been silent.

"Maybe he learned his lesson?"

Leo suddenly gets to his feet and clears his throat.

"Excuse me, mate." His voice wavers off down the carriage.

New Angus turn in his seat and Leo's stomach surges with panic. He's got no idea what he's going to say.

The moment hangs.

"Excuse me...mate?" Leo says again, louder. He's standing up in his seat.

New Angus also gets to his feet mirroring Leo.

"Me?" New Angus says, frowning.

"Yeah."

"Angus, right?" Leo says. "That's your name?"

New Angus's frown deepens.

"Er..." New Angus cocks his head on one side and says, "Do I know you, bro?"

Same accent, same exact voice, same irritable entitlement.

But this time something's missing. Leo can't put his finger on what.

"Um, yeah, sorry," Leo says, "but did you not just get off at the last stop?"

The words flutter out into the open. Leo feels like an idiot.

"I'm sorry?"

"It's just...if you did, you know this train is going north, right," Leo says. "This is the same one you were on before."

Leo tails off. New Angus is still looking at him, his face flat and unreadable.

The train turns a corner and both Leo and New Angus grip onto the heads of the chairs in front of them, swaying slightly.

It must just be the distance, the space between them, the night, the light, the weirdness of this situation but for a couple of terrible seconds, all Leo can see are two black voids where this iteration of Angus's eyes should be.

He drops his gaze, but Angus does not.

You're seeing things.

"You're going the wrong way, you know," Jodie says.

Jodie stands up and her voice is firm. Leo and New Angus both turn to her and Leo hears Jodie's very slight intake of breath as this Angus turns his dead eyes on her.

"Excuse me?" There is laughter now, unbridled in Angus voice. His face creases in a smirk. "What are you guys talking about? Are you fucking with me?"

"This train's going north," Jodie says. "Out into the sticks. Where are you headed? Ellie Hill? Malacstone?"

Another eerie quiet save for the rattle of the carriage. Leo's holding his breath.

"What are you talking about?" Angus says, and his voice is just a normal, human voice. His eyes are just normal, human eyes.

"I think," Jodie says, and now she falters, "I think…you're going the wrong way."

New Angus tears his eyes away from Jodie and looks down at his phone.

"You're joking?" he says. "Fuck's sake."

He turns and plonks himself back down, scrolling furiously.

Leo wants to say *well done* but he's not exactly sure what Jodie has done yet. Jodie sits back down, and Leo joins her.

"It's not right," she says. Her face is pale. She nods toward the back of her seat, "*He's* not right."

Leo doesn't like this. He wants to close his eyes until it's all over. Suddenly, new Angus's voice breaks the eerie quiet.

"Hello? Mum? Yeah, it's me." He's irritated, snappy. "No, I'm on the wrong fucking *train*. Going fucking *north*. I didn't realise you could get fucking *north* of here."

Leo turns to Jodie with a sigh of relief, eyes already rolling. It *is* Angus. Somehow, it doesn't matter how, but it's him, back on the train.

"What a fucking idiot," Leo mutters and tries to laugh.

Jodie doesn't return the laughter. Her face is pointed, suspicious.

Leo mouths, *what?* That sounds like Angus, it looks like Angus, it doesn't matter how he got here, but it's him alright.

"Something's not right," Jodie says. "This is fucking weird." It's like that mark on the window that was definitely just a bird strike. Two bird strikes at the same time."

That *definitely* wasn't hands.

Angus has dropped his voice, and Leo can't hear him over the rumble of the train.

"The guy is an idiot," Leo says to Jodie. "It's fine. He probably caught another train and got off at the wrong stop."

"How could he have caught a train?" Jodie says in a frantic little whisper. "There's only one line up here. If he did, it would have somehow had to be able to magically overtake this one."

Jodie's right.

"Something's wrong," she repeats, more to herself this time. "This doesn't make sense."

Beep-beep-boop-boop!

Leo and Jodie whip around. The sound is so obviously behind them now.

Jodie leaps up from her seat and strides through the carriage to the very end and starts rummaging on the seats that surround a plastic table. Leo looks at Angus. One elbow sticking out into the aisle, one foot tapping impatiently. One strap of his green rucksack hanging down from the baggage rack.

Just like before.

"Budge up."

Jodie has returned.

Leo shifts back into his seat beside the window and Jodie clambers back beside him.

"Look," she says, opening one hand, holding it low against her lap.

Leo peers and gasps.

It's a phone.

Not a smart phone but an old Nokia.

Leo reaches out a finger and points at the little screen, lit in a green glow.

"Where did you..."

(DON'T) CALL MUM

"Just shoved between the seat and the window over there." Jodie points her thumb backwards. "We must have missed it."

Leo knows he looked there at least twice but he doesn't say anything.

"It'll be locked," Jodie says. "We'll need a..."

But they won't need anything. The phone is unlocked. The little green screen shows the time, the signal and a little envelope icon. A number one and a three. Thirteen messages.

"Weird," Jodie says. "Maybe we should..."

Leo pauses.

Maybe they shouldn't.

"I'm not sure," Leo says, wary.

"I don't know." Jodie reaches for the phone but then pulls her hand back as if it's hot.

Reading someone's messages is such an invasion of privacy. Leo wonders what he would do if someone went through his phone.

But this plastic brick just doesn't carry the same resonance as a smart phone.

Jodie sighs. She leans over to look at Angus. "I just don't like it."

Something's not right.

Leo can't deny he can feel it too, no matter how much he doesn't want to. He holds the phone up and they both stare at it.

And then Leo wonders about the woman in the beige coat from before; did they see her get out at Darkton at all? Something in Leo wants her to come back in, to see Angus, this new Angus, to wonder who he is, to wonder what he is.

The Gangral always comes for naughty little boys like you.

But what is he going to do? Run through the carriages searching for her, begging her to tell him what she thinks?

He's not even sure he knows what *he* thinks.

Leo wants to ask Jodie what she *really* thinks. What does she mean when she says that something is wrong.

He's fumbling for the right words but then he hears it.

Beep-beep-boop-boop!

Leo cries out and nearly drops the phone. It buzzes slightly in his hand like the death throes of some bulging insect. Leo instinctively looks around the carriage. Angus glares their way. Leo watches him turn back slowly to his own screen.

(DON'T) CALL MUM

Jodie's fingers are bent into claws like a cat, arched on high alert.

Leo looks down. The phone is in his hand, but it doesn't feel like his hand. He feels like a million miles away.

Leo taps a button and the screen changes to the contents of the latest text.

From: Mum

> Call me asap

> Mum x

Relief.

It pours into his heart, warm and delicious, slicing through his fear, his worry, his apprehension. There's something about such a familiar message. Maybe it's how she's signed it 'Mum'.

Leo feels all the tightness inside him dissolve. He's not sure why this message has smoothed away his fears, maybe because it's the sort of thing his own mam would do sat on the edge of the sofa with her phone cradled in her left palm, right index finger pecking at the screen. Brow furrowed, glasses on.

Call me

Asap

Mum x

Leo taps the buttons with his thumb. He's slow with its interface. This stalwart of his own past which is now a relic. He smiles, wondering if in a few years, these sorts of phones will be back in fashion just like the baggy combat pants and band T-shirts of the 90s.

He brings up the message inbox, and his smile falls from his face.

Thirteen messages received.

Leo clicks through.

All the messages are from a single sender: Mum.

Call me

Asap

Mum x

Again and again and again. Leo desperately wants this to be funny, wants it to be the ignorance of an older generation, the distorted desperation of a mother.

But there are too many messages for it to be funny.

Leo wants to close the phone and throw it. Push it out of the train window like its contaminated, diseased.

Never speak of it again.

"You're not replying, are you?" Jodie pulls further away. He's already composing the message before his brain instructs him to stop (or before he screams).

(DON'T) CALL MUM

Hi, your son must have left his phone on a train but I've found it – if you let me know where you live

But then Leo stops typing.

Something's not right.

"Wait a sec, ok?" Jodie stares down at the message, the screen bright. "Don't do it yet."

She looks to the window and Leo follows her gaze to the smudge of mud, the bird strike from before.

Gan-gral-gan-gral.

Could Mr. Black contact a member of train staff please...Mr. Black, thank you

And now here's Angus, inexplicably back, impossibly back.

Stay away from Underwood.

Leo's instinct is to call out again, to ask new Angus whether he's lost his phone. His mouth, however, won't form those words. There's something about this phone, that's pulling him, compelling him.

The thirteen messages.

It's the kiss at the end of each one.

Mum x

This phone is the second least normal thing on this train right now.

Leo looks at Jodie

"I don't…I just think you should leave it. Give it to the guard or something."

"Why?" he asks, a laugh of uncertainty bleating out.

Leo knows why. He knows why because he also can't find the words to explain why. Something to do with the fear he used to feel late at night when the dark sprouted eyes and fingers crept around outside his window. He knows why because there's something about this stretch of emptiness between broken pit villages that pucker the darkness; there's something about the blood that soaks this land; Syrian mercenaries with bows, Roman legionaries with spears on endless marches through the driving rain. Witch-talk is all, *Salem, Salem, Salem* but no one ever mentions…

What does it look like, mam?

The only people who know that, son, are the ones what don't come back.

There's something in these haunted shores and tangled woods where Pan moves his tongue between the trees and the music of his pipes dance with a chill breeze down the blank, rain-washed scree.

This forgotten coast.

Could Mr. Black contact a member of train staff please. Mr. Black, thank you

A Pale Horseman high on the hills

(DON'T) CALL MUM

If you feel his hand in yours on some lonely road, he'll take you
Gan-gral, gan-gral
Gan-gral
Gan

Long Past Darkton
Long into the North

Leo opens up the phone's contacts.

There's only one.

Leo presses the call button.

Calling: mum

He can hear Jodie saying something beside him, her voice rising like a long-buried scream. But there's a ringtone, again and again, an electronic purr like night's cold hand reaching out across the world.

There's a moment of silence.

Then the call is answered.

Leo opens his mouth, anticipating a voice but instead there's a sudden, unnerving sensation of being squashed.

"What's..." Leo says and grunts as he's pressed against the window, the cool metal of the window frame against one arm.

There's someone between them on the seat.

Leo can't bear to look.

In the carriage window, he can see a blurry shape between Jodie and him, seemingly arriving between them as if it's crawling from underneath the seat.

A child that's pushed between its parents for comfort.

Like Leo pushed against mam when she lay on his bed and read to him at night.

The hole inside him, the hole between them where dad should have been.

The hole where the dark got in.

This is no child.

Leo breathes in the smell of deodorant or cologne. Something designer. He feels tough quads pushing against the outside of his own, a knee pressing against his knee.

Nike crew socks.

A large, cool hand sliding into his.

A curl of blond hair brushing his temple with such delicate motion and Leo feels a scream building.

A voice speaks but this voice isn't Angus; it's the distant, tinny voice of a voice on the other end of a phone.

Leo turns as Angus' hand holds his own in a terrible, crushing grip. The whites of Angus' eyes are the baleful terror of an animal muscled into sight of the abattoir blade. With his other hand, Angus holds up his phone to Leo, blocking out the rest of the carriage.

Leo can see the single word on the phone's screen

Mum

"Don't worry," a voice whispers. It's the pitch of a child, but the line is heavy with interference, as if the very timbre is causing it.

Leo gasps. He can't turn his eyes away. He can feel that crackling static infecting his own mind.

The voice comes again, whispering from a shriek of white noise. Digital fog.

"Don't worry. We'll help you find your mum."

Leo tries to close his eyes, his jaw grinding with another blast of static. He wants to look to Jodie, to his own mam, for someone to tell him none of this is real, that it's all some terrible dream and he'll wake up as the train finally pulls into Malacstone station and he's home at last.

But instead, with a sensation not unlike the sudden plunging feeling when one finally drops into deep sleep.

Leo's sanity cascades into a long, black tunnel with the speed of a train, racing through the night.

North
Far, Far From Home

You're standing at the very end of Underwood's platform where a wire mesh fence holds back a tumble of green thrashing in the rain and the wind.

There was never a horseman.

Never a blurred figure moving toward you down the hill in little bursts like rain trickling down a window.

Pale skin. Two black eyes. Boreholes staring into you. Through you.

A faded lager can crumpled on the path leads into the village; a clump of dandelions; the tarmac ridges and split as if some vast serpent once writhed beneath it.

Somewhere ahead a car hisses by. Lights cut through the rain.

There's a building, a sign. A bus stop and shutters on a shop. Normal things that smooth over the sight of half-dreamed horseman that could easily be that discarded umbrella tattered like the wing of a bat.

There's a wall, a fence, a sign that reads: *Sky Sports*.

It's the Black Bull.

It's normal.

You sigh with relief and step forward. It might be weird up here but it's the North.

You pull out your phone and grin down at it, your teeth illuminated by another passing car. You don't even mind the spray of puddle-water against your jacket because it makes everything a bit more real.

You open your contacts and find 'mum'. You can see light in the pub windows, you anticipate the smell of the place, hops and old fryer oil. The toilets will have one wall, a vast porcelain urinal with yellow lemon-scented cakes clustered at one end. There might even be a room with a bed with a too-tight sheet, the faint surge of black mould.

It's ringing.

The Black Bull, Underwood. That's where you are. You're about to cross the road when she picks up.

"Hello?"

"Mum." You almost bend double with relief. "Jesus, I've finally found civilisation."

There's a silence and you check the screen, the bars filling up with signal.

"Hello?" Her voice sounds faraway, and this lands hard. You imagine her in the living room, at the end of the sofa; dad won't even look up from *The Telegraph*.

"Mum? It's me. You know, Angus. Your only son."

Another silence.

"Jesus, mum. Have you got your phone the right way around?"

Your laughter clatters out onto the road. No more cars and you cross over, the Black Bull up ahead.

No sign of the horseman.

The horseman that was never there.

"I'm sorry…" Mum's voice is quiet, confused. "I can't…"

"Hang on." You step over a puddle, make for the front steps of the pub. Faux lanterns jut from the wall with a sign for a beer garden. "Signal will be better here."

"Who is it, love?" Faint, gruff.

You feel your face scowl at dad's words.

"Mum…hello? Hello? Can you hear me?"

There's another infuriating silence. You step into the doorway of the Black Bull. Maybe it's the rain fucking with your phone. You don't sound like yourself, perhaps?

Is that a sob?

There's a rustling and mum's voice gets muffled, but you can still hear her.

"I don't know…no…he said we have a *son*!"

"Mum?"

More rustling and dad's voice again. Irritated. He'll have laid his paper down over his knees and his thatch of eyebrows will have creased.

"Just hang up. It'll be one of those Indian scams."

Mum comes back on the line.

"Not today, thank you," she says, officious.

"Mum!" You try and laugh but it catches in your throat. "It's me. It's Angus. Listen, I got the wrong train. I'm in some place out in the middle of fuck-knows-where. It's a village called Underwood up in Northumberland. I'm at a pub. It's…"

"Angus?" Mum sounds horribly old, suddenly ancient, confused and you get a little flash of fear in your chest.

"Yeah!" you say. "Me! Are you ok?"

More silence.

"I said, *hang up*!"

Dad again. The fear is becoming a terrible, leaden panic.

"Mum? It's me, Angus. Are you ok? I'm stuck…I need…"

"Angus…" Mum's voice creaks like a rusty hinge. "He says he's called *Angus*."

Dad makes a harrumphing sound and tells her to *just hang the thing up for God's sake*.

You want to laugh, to congratulate them on their joke, because this is what it is. Just a silly joke. Just mum and dad messing with you.

But mum and dad never mess with you. They never have and never will.

Mum comes back on the line. You hear her clear her throat. A high-pitched, scraping sound.

"You sound like a lovely young man," she says, her voice strained and curt.

"Mum..." It falls from you in a whisper.

"But you need to find yourself a better job. Stop bothering people in the middle of the night."

Your lips can only open and close.

There's a moment when you hear dad starting to speak again.

"Hang the bloody..."

The line goes dead.

You stand there in the doorway of the pub. You're on the stone steps, staring down into your phone.

Everything's red.

You try out a laugh. Push it into the night because this must be a joke.

You call back.

Nothing.

Not even a ringtone.

She's blocked your number.

This sinks in as you turn back and look at the way you have come. You look at the deserted road and the path that leads to the train station and the white metal sign that reads, 'Underwood'. You stare out further to the hills and the forests.

Nothing moves save for the rattle of the rain.

You try mum again, again, again, eventually cracking your phone screen with your finger and collapsing into a ball on the steps of the pub, sobs shaking you. Sorrow bubbling up and slipping its hands into a sudden, stark terror. The pair dancing with frozen feet against your heart.

This can't be real.

When you stand up, the rain has stopped.

The night, however, is still going strong.

You're soaking wet and you begin to shiver.

The village of Underwood is still. The trees and lampposts drip silent tears into petrol-patterned puddles.

The pub door, where there was once a window is boarded up with moss-ridden panels of MDF. Those lamps on the wall are dead eyes and the smell of hops and old carpet is a foetid reek of creeping time.

You jolt at the sudden, acrid stink of piss and stagger back, nearly falling. The Black Bull is dark and dead, snuffed out, black as the wick of a candle in the gloom. Ragged rafters bulge like burned bones above. Roof slates like cracked coffin lids scattered on the path.

Wooden lids nailed over long-broken windows; a ragged edge of glass peeping out from between them. Sly and uncaring.

A curl of dead ivy.

Scorched stone.

The only other building is the shop you saw earlier, a metal grate pulled down and rusted closed. Above it, the windows in the flat above are grey and cracked. An 'o' of a single stone through the glass. Weeds reach from the cracks in the road.

Silence swells here between the remains of this place as the night rides on through.

What are you going to do?

What the fuck are you going to do?

"Don't worry."

You jump at the voice, crying out, sending a bird clattering from the sodden eaves of the burnt-out pub.

You whip around.

"Who's there?" You swing your fists at the silence.

You slump, panting, all the energy gone. Your clothes cling to you like a shroud.

"Don't worry." It's closer now.

"Who's there?" You scream, the back of your throat suddenly raw. Your mouth suddenly dry.

When the small hand slips as if from nowhere into yours. When the icy little fingers curl around, you feel like you have no more strength to resist.

"Don't worry," comes the voice, a little voice, a child's voice from near, from far, from the empty streets to the great rearing hills in the distance. A pale rider waits at the bottom of the hill.

But the voice is all sibilants as if there are too many teeth in a too-small mouth.

You turn to look.

"We'll help you find your mam…"

Acknowledgements

The support of friends and family is always huge in the throes of creating a book from the seed of a strange idea. However, I must first credit the inspiration for this story: the loud woman who plopped herself down opposite me on a train about fifteen years ago. You stared out the window, a scowl on your face and at the top of your voice, declared, 'God! The north is such a fah-king *dump!*' into your phone.

Wherever you are today, we're happier up here without you and I hope you never meet a Gangral.

The writing of this book couldn't have happened without the following people: Sarah and Harry. You're the ones who tolerate me sitting up in the attic all day making stuff up and getting mad with myself when it doesn't quite go to plan. Your love, support and belief in me has never wavered. All of what I do is for you both.

My tireless agent Sandra Sawicka for your constant encouragement and dedication to pushing everything I create to the next level.

Ariell at Wild Hunt Books for making the smoothing, un-knotting and editing process of *(Don't) Call*

Mum such an enjoyable one. And Luísa Dias for the phenomenal front cover. I'm looking forward to reading all the other Northern Weird Project books!

To my friends, Paul, Jess and Aurelia. Your love and company are worth more than any of you know. Richard 'Meat Consultant' Dawson; we're coming up to 30 years of friendship now. Putting up with me in your life for that long surely is deserving of a medal! Thank you for not just all the music, movies, games of FIFA and dumplings in the Grainger Market, but the time you took to offer such valuable thoughts and insight during the writing of this book.

To Everyone who has asked for a signature, a photo, or has come over for a chat at an event. It's all massively appreciated. Huge props must go to the book bloggers, bookstagrammers and various other social media folk who have shown such unyielding support for me and my weird books. I am eternally in your debt.

Lastly, thank *you* for being here and reading all the way to the very last word. Let's meet again sometime soon...

About the Author

Matt Wesolowski is an author from Newcastle-Upon-Tyne in the UK. He is a former English teacher for young people in the PRU and care systems. Matt was a winner of the Pitch Perfect competition at the Bloody Scotland Crime Writing Festival in 2015. His debut thriller, *Six Stories*, was an Amazon bestseller in the USA, Canada, the UK and Australia, and a WHSmith Fresh Talent pick. *Hydra*, was published in 2018 and became an international bestseller. *Changeling*, the third book in the series, was published in 2019 and was longlisted for the Theakston's Old Peculier Crime Novel of the Year. His fourth book, *Beast*, won the Amazon Publishing Readers' Independent Voice Book of the Year award in 2020 and was followed by *Deity* and then *Demon* in 2022. The *Six Stories* series is currently being adapted for television. Matt currently works as a tutor for Faber Academy. He lives in Newcastle with his partner and son, several tanks of rescued goldfish, a snake and a cat and an axolotl.

About The Northern Weird Project

This book is a part of The Northern Weird Project by Wild Hunt Books, a collection of six pocket-sized novellas by authors who are writing and living in the North of England.

Incorporating eerie and uncanny incidents, these novellas investigate aspects of the North through setting, subject and character.

All books in this series are available to order from our bookshop.
https://www.wildhuntbooks.co.uk/bookshop

More From The Northern Weird Project

This House Isn't Haunted But We Are
by Stephen Howard

Simon and Priya's young daughter has died in a tragic accident. Determined to heal their fracturing marriage, the couple move to the North Yorkshire Moors to renovate a dilapidated rural cottage. However, they just can't process their grief as increasingly eerie events unfold. A child's ghostly figure appears on the moors, doors lock themselves, and a mysterious stain grows from the loft. Is it their daughter haunting them or something else?

The Off-Season
by Jodie Robins

It's the off-season in the seaside resort town of Blackpool, where Tommy never imagined he would return. His relationship has broken down, so he returns home to keep an eye on his widowed father. While counting down the hours before attending the funeral of a well-loved friend, a mysterious group turns up on the seafront. One by one, the locals are entranced by their presence until Tommy and his father can no longer resist the allure. Tommy soon discovers a secret desire his father has been harbouring for his entire life.

The Retreat
by Gemma Fairclough

Richard's sister Julie returns home from a mysterious wellness facility in remote Cumbria in 1994. He's convinced that this place was a cult and was the cause of his sister's eventual suicide. Finally, after years as an unaccomplished academic, he decides to investigate the disturbing accusations against the Hartman Retreat Centre. Then he meets Lucy, a young woman whose story is eerily similar to his sister's decades before. Richard is determined to unearth what's really been happening at the Hartman Retreat Centre but more importantly, who is Charles Hartman, the celebrated healer who casts a powerful hold over all who come to the retreat.

Good Boy

by Neil McRobert

After a boy vanishes on the outskirts of a small Northern town, a woman spies from her window a mysterious man digging a grave in the exact spot of the disappearance. However, when she confronts him, the man's true purpose is far more chilling than she could have imagined and the history of the town's fatal past unfolds. What has been hiding in this small northern town all these years? A gripping story of supernatural horror, nostalgia and mystery.

Turbine 34

by Katherine Clements

It's 2035 and England is experiencing the hottest summer in living memory. A 61-year-old environmental scientist, is tasked with evaluating the impact of a controversial new wind farm on the West Yorkshire moors. Camped out alone at Turbine 34 which was built on the ancient peat bog, she soon discovers signs of the devastation caused by the construction, she begins to see things that shouldn't be there. She has dedicated her life to protecting the moor, but will it protect her?

Wild Hunt Books would like to thank the following Lifetime Supporters:

Daniel Sorabji
Jan Penovich
Blaise Cacciola

BECOME A SUPPORTER BY CONTACTING US AT

INFO@WILDHUNTBOOKS.CO.UK

The Publisher would also like to thank the following early supporters of The Northern Weird Project:

Aidan Smith
Alex Herod
Ali W
Alicia Lomas-Gross
Anthony Martin
Beth Baskett
Bethany Vare
Blair Rose
Carmen
Charlotte Platt
Charlotte Tierney
Emma Armshaw
Freya S
George Dunn
Heidi Marjamäki
Ianthe May
J. Aaron Courts CWO4, USMC, Retired
Jeff
Jennifer B. Lyday
K. Wicks
Kelsey Stoddard
Kirsty Logan

Laura Elliott
Lisa Elliott
Lynne G
Mandy Bublitz
Mark Taylor
Martyn Waites
Monica Voynovska
Nicola Leedham
Nina Woodcock
Rachel Bridgeman
Rosie Warfield
Samuel Best
Sheena E. Perez
Sonja Zimmermann
Sophy Holland
Stefanie Olivola
Stephanie Eleanor Henrichs Welch
Stewart Mack
Vince Fairclough

www.ingramcontent.com/pod-product-compliance
Ingram Content Group UK Ltd.
Pitfield, Milton Keynes, MK11 3LW, UK
UKHW030914120525
5857UKWH00002B/135

9 781739 458041